Spirals

-

Deadly Memories

Amanda Glenn

ISBN13:-9781892076472
ISBN:10-1892076470

For: M, J, C, and C.

Note:

Switzerland is a real place. All other places, people, and events in this book are fictitious amalgams – products of the author's over active imagination. Any resemblance to actual persons, living or dead, events or locals is extremely coincidental.

Author photo: Karen Praxel
Cover photo: Eugene Budinger

CHAPTER 1

Must have hit my head.

Her fingers felt the goose egg above her left eye and rubbed at crinkly flakes of dried blood, scrubbing to get them off. She checked to see if there was any blood still oozing from the wound. Her fingers came away clean.

Well, how did you do that?

First things first, where are you?

In a squash field.

In a ditch next to a squash field, she corrected, looking about.

More precisely she was in a ditch between a gravel road and what she took to be several acres of zucchini. Across the way a stark cube of a two-story house, its metal roll-down shutters closed tight, looked unwelcoming among tidy rows of grapevines. At her feet a bicycle lay in an abandoned heap.

I fell off the bicycle.

Did you break something?

She moved – tentative – rising slowly to her feet. Nothing hurt but her head.

Guess not.

She pulled the bike upright and inspected it for damage. It was ancient – rusty red with balloon tires and a wide seat like the one she'd had when she was twelve. It didn't look broken. Wheeling it back onto the road, she looked both ways.

"Was I coming or going?" she wondered aloud.

Which way is home?

Good question.

Neither way looked the least bit familiar. Panic rose in her chest, she could feel her heart thumping.

Think, she demanded, gripping the handlebars as if she were afraid the bike was going to take off without her.

Where were you going?

Hastily she checked the pockets of her gray, zip up, hooded sweatshirt. They were empty. So were the pockets of her Levi's. She noted they were not new, snug fitting, but comfortable. She had to look down to see she was also wearing a red turtleneck knit shirt and a pair of white leather sneakers. The panic reasserted itself.

Who am I? Where was I going?

Left and right, in the distance, there were trees, roof tops. Smoke curled lazily from a chimney to the right and she was drawn there, then, looking back, she caught sight of a black sedan making the turn onto the road just beyond the trees to the left and turned the front wheel of the bike.

Do I know that car? Maybe someone was coming to look for her.

Hesitant, she put her left foot on the bike pedal, shoved off and surprised herself by agilely swinging her right leg over the seat. She pedaled easily toward the black car, which now sped toward her, and raised a hand to wave as it neared. The vehicle did not slow, nor even give way in acknowledgement of her existence on the narrow roadway. Only a hasty dismount as she swung to the grassy verge saved her from another sprawl into the ditch.

"Rude!"

Very rude.

From the passenger seat a darkly handsome man looked back at her, his eyes made contact and flickered, then he turned back toward the driver. Neither man in the back seat gave her so much as a glance. A cold chill ran through her, she knew the man in the passenger seat, she was sure of it, though a name would not come.

She wheeled the bike back on the road and headed right, toward the smoking chimney. The left no longer felt friendly.

How do you know you had a bicycle like this?
I know, that's all. I just know.

The bike picked up speed as she pedaled energetically toward the unknown. Tall trees loomed ahead, perhaps a quarter of a mile on, behind them she could see a large stone building.

The chateau.

Could be, could be a chateau.

You thought the black car was familiar.

She slowed.

What are you going to do when you get there?

Walk up to the door and knock.

And say what?

Excuse me, do you know who I am.

An internal argument was taking place.

Terrific, maybe it's an insane asylum and I'm an escapee.

There was a gentle curve to the road, as she cleared it she could see that it continued, straight as an arrow, past the "chateau". Beyond the stone building there appeared to be an intersection, and she could see the superstructure of a bridge ahead on her left. It looked like a railway bridge. Then she saw the river, a serious waterway that circled in to run parallel to the road and consequently under the bridge.

She was almost upon him before she spotted the man standing in the road next to the medieval stone structure she was unreasonably sure was a chateau and a place she should know. One that should know her.

The man was handsome. Tall, sandy hair, nice shoulders, trim. Blue eyes she noted as she stopped before him. He looked a little perturbed.

"That was a long ride. I was beginning to worry."

He looked at her closer.

"What did you do to yourself? Did you fall?"

"I... I think so."

"Think so? Come on. Let's get you a nice cup of Marta's coffee and have a look at that bump."

"Marta?"

With my luck that will be his wife.

7

Wedding ring. A quick glance confirmed it.

"She's been busy baking again. More of those jam filled cookies you like."

"Mmmh," she said, allowing him to take the bike from her and followed behind into the small courtyard. It looked sort of familiar.

Everything looks sort of familiar.

Ask.

Tell.

Say something!

The three tiers of triple arches between the round tower and the three-story squared end of the building blurred and then spun.

"I don't think I feel well."

To prove it she fainted, falling in a heap on the ancient stones.

"Taylor. Darling, wake up. Marta, is the doctor coming?"

The words came through a dense fog that muddled her thoughts and made her eyelids too heavy to lift.

"Taylor!"

It was a male voice. Worried. Nice though, she decided.

Who do you suppose Taylor is?

He's talking to you, you ninny.

I am not a ninny.

The question is, are you Taylor?

"Umphuh," she mumbled and with great effort forced her eyelids open.

The handsome man was bent close, the blue eyes staring, anxious, and caring. The caring part sparked a warm response in her.

What a nice man.

"My head hurts," she said, trying to sit up.

"We've called a doctor," he explained. "You must have taken a tumble."

"Landed in the ditch," she said, nodding then was sorry she had as a sharp pang stabbed through the back of her skull.

"Do you need one of your pills?" he asked.

"I... please." He looked so familiar.

The black car looked familiar.

She was reluctant to tell him she hadn't the least idea who he was. He left the room. To get the pills she supposed, hoping it would be a prescription bottle with a label. Then, at minimum, she would know her own name. She looked around. It was a big room. Stone walls. High, timbered ceilings. A small fire burned brightly in the age-blackened hearth. The fireplace itself was huge, the kind one cooked in in the Middle-Ages. On either side of the fireplace windows — narrow and tall with tiny, glittering panes above wooden window seats — let in pale light. On the far right of the same wall there was a massive iron bound plank door, the one the man had gone through. She lay on a purple plush sofa, overstuffed, the kind her mother had when she was in elementary school.

How do you know that?

I do, don't argue.

She craned her neck and saw there was plenty of room behind the divan for anyone entering through the door to pass, there was even a massive sideboard behind her against the stone wall. Above the sideboard hung a mirror in a gilt frame. A matching purple chair was at right angles to the sofa with a small table between, and across from where she lay was a long dining table with benches down the sides and heavy, knobby, high backed arm chairs at either end. A bouquet of yellow and white flowers in a blue patterned pitcher sat among the glass cruets on the tabletop. On the wall behind the table, a tapestry, ten by twenty or larger, depicted a hunting scene in time muted colors. On the floor a red carpet, ageless, from ancient Persia, or maybe the local Wal-Mart, stretched before the hearth between the table and the sitting area and lent warmth and color. Opposite the fireplace, at the back of the cavernous room, was a low counter and behind that a kitchen. A perfectly modern — cream woodwork, acres of glass faced cupboards, microwave, wall oven, gray granite countertops — enormous kitchen. In this semi-shabby, fairytale space it was a shock.

You were surprised the first time you saw it.

How...

Never mind.

A timer dinged and a sturdy woman of indeterminate years came out of a door at the left end of the long counter which, it seemed, was really an island. She crossed to the oven and withdrew a sheet of cookies, the hot almond-vanilla aroma wafting across the room like a siren's call. Bright light from the one tiny window in the back wall of the kitchen glinted off her white cap of soft curls.

"The doctor will be here any minute."

She had a pleasant accent.

"I promised him coffee. Would you prefer tea?"

"I..."

What do I like?

"Coffee would be fine, thank you."

CHAPTER 2

Taylor Robbins. That's what the name on the label said.

Sounds like a man's name.

Sounds nice.

I like it.

This is serious heart medication!

Did I have a heart attack?

Stroke. It would have been a stroke.

Yeah, but did I have one?

"Taylor? Aren't you going to take one? Would you like some water? You don't usually..."

"I was going to wait for my coffee," Taylor said. "I.. I'm not so sure I need one right now after all."

"Good," he said, sounding relieved. "So, what happened?"

"Not really sure.."

There was a knock at the door and Marta — that was who Taylor decided the white-haired woman was — went to open it.

The doctor was young. Taylor had to stifle the urge to ask him just exactly how long he'd been practicing.

I have children older.

And you know this how?

The doctor spoke stilted English, unaccompanied by the stereotypical use of hands even when he rattled on in Italian with Marta. He examined Taylor's head, checked her eyes with a tiny penlight, checked her pulse, and her blood pressure, then listened to her heart, raising concerned eyes to meet hers.

Taylor handed him the bottle of pills, he read the label and nodded understanding.

"A mild concussion," he said, handing back the plastic container. "How did you do this, Signora?"

Signora? Am I married?

Who to?

A quick check of her hand confirmed the wedding band and a sizable turquoise and diamond ring.

11

"I have no idea. I mean I must have been riding the bicycle and fallen. In the squash field. In the ditch by the squash field, I was in the ditch. I don't remember."

"Taylor, darling," the blue-eyed, sandy-haired man said, leaning forward from his seat in the purple chair.

Him?

I should be so lucky.

I don't believe it.

Why not?

"I don't remember a thing. Not how I got in the ditch. Not who I am. Where I am. Nothing," Taylor got out in a gush and burst into tears. "The label on the bottle says Taylor Robbins, but I don't know if that's me. I don't remember."

"Signora," the doctor soothed, patting her hand.

"Darling," the tall man cooed.

"Ahh," Marta said, setting a tray on the table. "It must be frightening, though there have been times when I thought forgetting everything would be a blessing."

She handed Taylor a small cup filled with hot black coffee, the aroma so heady it was a caffeine fix in itself.

"Thank you," Taylor said and started to lift it to her lips.

"You like cream. I'll get it."

He — the maybe husband — sprang from his chair.

"I do?"

Taylor felt mildly annoyed that this tall man knew more about her than she did about herself.

"Does she need to go the hospital?" he asked, crossing to the table.

"No. I think not. I will leave my home number, but it is a very slight concussion. Now is just the trauma. She will remember. Answer her questions but do not push. Yes? Let her remember at her own pace. I will come back in two days. On Thursday."

He accepted his cup of coffee and one of the warm cookies with a rush of warm Italian words that made Marta beam.

Taylor accepted a cookie and nibbled on it wishing the doctor were taking her with him.

You aren't expected to know anyone in a hospital.

Scaredy cat!

Got that right. What do I know about these people?

They look nice.

He looks delicious.

How do I know he didn't push me into the ditch?

Great, now I'm paranoid.

Wonder if that's new?

"Thursday morning about ten?"

The doctor asked, looking from Taylor to the man to Marta.

"You will save me another pastry, yes?"

Taylor shrugged, the man nodded and Marta continued to beam.

"The Signora may sleep, but not too long at first. You will wake her every two hours tonight. After that is OK."

Sleep did sound like a good idea. Taylor felt a good nap was due.

Maybe this was all a bad dream.

I could wake up and know who I am.

Or not.

"Could I take a nap now?" Taylor asked. "I do feel tired."

"Of course, Signora. A short one. Until Thursday then."

The doctor smiled at her and nodded his head respectfully at Marta, shook the tall man's hand and left.

"I... where... I don't remember where my room is."

"I'll take you up," the maybe husband said, offering a hand to steady her rise from the sofa.

Taylor wanted to remember his name. She tried a dozen or so mentally but none sparked recognition.

"Thank you," she said turning to Marta. "The cookies — pastries — are delicious. I really liked the filling."

13

Marta smiled at her but her eyes seemed clouded with concern.

I bet I said that before.

This is just too weird.

Marta followed them to the door and out onto the wide porch with its worn stone floor and the stone domes in the ceiling that gave it a Moorish feel. "Signore Chris, there will be four for lunch?"

Chris! His name is Chris. That's right.

As in Christopher.

As in Christopher Robbins!

I'm Mrs. Christopher Robbins!

Winnie the Pooh thoughts threatened to make her giggle then she remembered the rest of what Marta had asked.

Four for lunch?

We have children?!

"I think so," Chris was saying. "Lars promised to be back and Laszlo can't sleep forever.

Lars and Laszlo!

Whatever was I thinking when I named them?

Family names?

Whose family?

She followed the man named Chris up a wide set of stone steps off the end of the porch climbing between the round tower and the bulk of the building. The stairs made a U-turn and narrowed before it emptied them out on to the second-floor balcony directly above the porch. Through the three stone arches she could see the courtyard below, a garden, and beyond that the road. The floor was stone and overhead stone domes matched the ones below.

To the side of the steps through a narrow arch Taylor spied another flight of stairs that led upward into darkness. Along the back wall of the balcony there were two massive doors, at least four by eight and made of wide planks strapped in metal and more reminiscent of dungeons (and fairy tales) than chateaux. At the far end of the balcony another door of similar proportion was filled with a pair of French doors whose wood frames bore a pristine cream paint finish. Through the doors Taylor glimpsed an inviting sitting room in shades of green.

Chris stopped at the second of the dungeon doors. "This is our room," he said pushing the door open and standing aside for her to enter.

"Oh!" Taylor squeaked, then with a covetous last look over her shoulder at the comforts promised at the end of the balcony entered, the term "our room" spinning out its probable meanings in glaring warning tones at the back of her mind.

It was a huge room, half the width of the great room downstairs, but like it, running fully through the building. There was a single tiny window in the far wall, its four little panes of glass casting prisms on floor and walls through their flawed but shiny clean faces. The long wall to the right was stone, the one to the left paneled in dark wood. Overhead, just as downstairs, great beams spanned the room, supporting the wide planks of the ceiling that she realized must be the floor of the rooms above. Two massive armoires sat along the wooden wall opposite the beds. Each bed, at least queen sized, had a large dresser between it and the outside wall it was nearest and a nightstand and lamp on its other side. Between the nightstands a burgundy velvet drape swagged from ceiling to floor and everywhere there were rugs, some more worn than others, all with assorted shades of burgundy the ground for patterns in jewel tones. At the foot of the near bed there was a bench upholstered in faded needlepoint, at the end of the far bed an immense brass bound, wooden chest that appeared to have been painted red at some point but now retained only dark hints of former splendor.

The bed linens, under a quilted crimson coverlet were white and bright and lace trimmed.

"Nice," Taylor said appreciatively.

"That's what you said the first time," Chris told her, closing the door.

"Well, then, I'm consistent." The big door did not look any less dungeon like from the inside despite the fact that an intricately carved door hid the small barred window. She wondered if he was going to lock her in.

"I feel kind of silly, wanting a nap before lunch."

"We were up early," he looked deep into her eyes and smiled as if he knew a secret. "And you had a big breakfast, then you wanted to ride the bicycle," he stopped talking to study her face again. "The doctor said we were supposed to let you remember on your own. But you have had a big morning, falling down and all. A good reason for a short rest. Get up on the bed and I'll take your shoes off for you."

Taylor noticed that the beds were tall, the kind you need a set of steps to get into. She found the steps hidden in the folds of the crimson bedskirt. The bed was firm at the core, wrapped in softness, and welcoming. She let her head sink back on the pile of feather pillows. Her eyes closed and she promised herself she would think this whole thing out later. She heard the first shoe hit the floor but not the second.

CHAPTER 3

"...not in his room. Did you check the bathroom?"

The voice was loud – Chris. Her husband. The idea amused her.

Who's missing?

"I've searched the chateau, all three floors."

A nice voice, warm, firm, a slight accent, more puzzled than anxious.

"Marta hasn't seen him."

"I was here with Taylor, perhaps he went for a walk," she heard Chris say.

"Emmhm." the other man seemed to agree. "Marta told me about the amnesia, that we're not to tell. You're right to keep a close eye on her. Laszlo will no doubt turn up for lunch."

"Either way no sense upsetting Taylor."

So, Laszlo is missing and not a child or surely they'd be more upset.

What aren't they supposed to tell?

Why would I be upset?

Taylor sat up and stretched. She heard the door open.

"Well, well. I was coming to wake you. Hungry?"

Chris smiled at her and her heart leapt.

How could I forget a man like that?!

"Here let me help you with your sneakers," he said, lifting them from the floor.

"I can do it," Taylor reassured him quickly. "I'm not an invalid."

"No, but you are beginning to resemble a casualty of war."

"Huh?"

"Better take your purse down with you and check out your face in the mirror. That's going to be some shiner."

"Oh," she said, touching the sore spot on her head. "Where's the bathroom?"

"First floor, in the tower."

17

Coming out onto the balcony Taylor looked around. To the left of the stairs there was an entrance to a tower room. A good ten feet in diameter, with a stone floor, the empty room had glassless, vertical slits — arrow slits, it came to her — for windows and no door. To the right of the stairs through an archway there was a short hall and steps leading up. Descending she found the third step before the bottom was wider, at the tower end there was a wooden door, two wide planks held together with iron banding, a wrought iron latch for a handle, and a round top.

"If it's open," Chris motioned to the door standing slightly ajar, "it's available. Lock it if you wish to be undisturbed, leave it open when you go. House rules. I'll be in there."

He pointed to a wall, behind which Taylor knew, lay the room where she'd seen the doctor.

"Oh my!" she exclaimed, seeing herself in the long mirror on the inside of the bathroom door. A purply tinge had spread across half of her face, darker, angrier looking on her forehead and in the hollow of her eye.

No amount of make-up is going to hide that.

Why try?

Vanity.

Take another good look, honey. Not much there to be vain about.

Taylor felt a knot in her chest. The face in the mirror looked old.

You just woke up.

You had an accident.

You look like hell.

You look like his mother.

Please, his big sister!

You don't look that bad.

You don't look that good.

"Would you all shut up," Taylor said, staring into her own face intently. "Whoever you are, now is no time to slip off the edge."

You're fine. Just watch and listen and wait to remember.

And don't trust anybody, a cynic voice within cautioned.

She looked with approval at the round room. White tile covered the walls to about six feet. There was a soak tub and next to that a glassed-in shower. The toilet was next to the shower and separated by a knee wall from the pedestal sink. The arrow slits were filled with red, yellow, and blue slashes of stained glass. Thick white towels were stacked on a stool against the wall and creamy yellow bath rugs hung over the edge of the tub and the shower door. Iron sconces, either side of the little gilt mirror over the sink, floated a round vanity light each and a large frosted globe hung by chain from a hook in middle of the stone domed ceiling.

Taylor brushed her short hair, put on some lipstick and smiled back at the pink and purple yin and yang of a face in the mirror. Curious, she checked out the purse. Besides the lipstick, some mascara, and eyeliner there was a change purse with Mexican, French, American, and Swiss coins. No driver's license but there was a passport, barely a year old, that indicated Taylor Robbins was an American citizen living in Mexico.

This is not Mexico.

Well, it's not Chicago.

Chicago! What made me think of Chicago?

I live, lived? — in Chicago.

Another fact regained.

So why am I living in Mexico?

"For that matter, what am I doing here, and where exactly is here?"

She left the bathroom being careful to leave the door ajar.

"Ah, there you are," Chris said as Taylor entered the large room. "Do you want wine, the doctor didn't say but..."

"I think not," Taylor said.

The table was set for lunch, five places.

19

"Who...?" she waved a hand at the table.

"You, me, Marta, and Lars and Laszlo. They're... business associates of mine," Chris explained.

"Chris?" Santa Claus in a khaki suit had opened the door and stepped part way in.

The voice seemed familiar.

The one you heard upstairs.

Taylor couldn't help staring. The man's white hair and beard, the amply padded large frame, even the twinkle in his eye cried out for a red plush suit and eight reindeer waiting with a sleigh in the drive. What she didn't understand was the flash of terror that melted as quickly as it came.

"Laszlo is still missing," Santa said. "I've looked again and..." he paused, looked at Taylor, then jerked his head, indicating, Taylor gathered, that Chris was to join him outside.

"Tell Marta we'll be right in. Her food is too good to let get cold," Chris said, with a charming little boy smile that brought a smile to Taylor's lips.

"I can see why I'd marry him," Taylor said as the door closed.

"Did you say something?" Marta asked, bringing a breadboard with two large crusty loaves and a wicked looking bread knife to the table.

"Just musing aloud," Taylor told her. "I must say I have great taste in husbands."

Marta laughed.

"Christopher Robbins is a very special man. Do you remember now?"

"No, not really. Bits and pieces past and present but none of it makes sense."

She smiled to relieve the concerned look that came over Marta's face.

"But my face looks worse than my head aches and my nose tells me there is a wonderful meal in store. I may not remember exactly why I'm here, or even where here is but I do know I'm hungry and I suspect I am a good eater."

She patted her slightly soft middle.

"You need to get another good look in that long mirror. Inventory.

She hoped the rest of her was in better shape. Taylor inspected the slender wrists extended from the pushed up sleeves of the red turtleneck and felt reassured.

"May I help?"

Marta and Taylor laded the table from a feast ready and waiting on the island. There was a great bowl of green salad, a second cutting board with three kinds of cheese, zucchini stewed with tomatoes and onions, whole carrots six to seven inches long, steaming hot and swimming in butter, ravioli in an herbed cream sauce, and a tremendous platter of grilled sausages and slices of roast meat. Pork, Taylor thought. She'd just placed a frosty pitcher of lemonade on the table when Chris and the man she surmised was Lars returned.

"Looks like Laszlo will miss a great meal," Chris said lightly.

"More for me," Santa/Lars rejoined, reaching the table and seating himself quickly in one of the armchairs.

Chris helped Taylor over the bench and dropped a quick kiss on her cheek before sitting down beside her. Marta joined them and after a second's silence rang a small silver bell Taylor had noticed among the cruets.

Grace.

Right. Family tradition.

Marta told you that the first evening.

And you remember!

Laszlo did not return during the meal. Chris and Lars became increasingly conscious of the time, checking their watches regularly though, Taylor noticed, it did not seem to dull either's appetite.

When the meal was finished Taylor helped clear away, moving dirty dishes and leftovers to the island without thinking why that that was as much aid as Marta would allow.

Stay on your side of the counter.

Another house rule.

Something else I remember.

So — while you're doing all this remembering — just where did you meet Chris?

How did you become Mrs. Robbins?

And who is Laszlo?

Why is he missing?

She felt arms come around her from behind and Chris nuzzled her neck.

"We have some appointments. I wouldn't suggest another ride on the bike but you have your book. It's nice in the garden."

"I'll be fine," Taylor assured him thinking that a closer inspection of her tote and maybe a look through her clothes and luggage would spur memories.

It was pleasant in the garden. An eclectic mix of vegetables, herbs, and well-established perennials, laced with pea gravel paths. A small stone structure, covered in pale yellow roses and a vine Taylor couldn't identify, separated the garden from the driveway.

A tool house.

Now. A cookhouse several hundred years ago. So the smell of food didn't annoy the fussy Italian who built the chateau.

Five hundred years plus.

Right!

Another piece of the near past slid into place. Taylor shifted slightly among the cushions on the painted wooden chaise under the rose covered eaves of the ancient cookhouse, the latest Anne Perry mystery face down in her lap. The sun was warm on her face, the mixed scents of the garden wrapped her. Behind the tool shed nee cookhouse the tall trees whispered softly in the breeze and dappled the light that fell across the cobbled drive and the road.

The search through her wallet and clothing after lunch had produced little. There were pictures of thirty and fortyish adults and cherubic children. They looked like nice people. Her children and grandchildren she assumed, feeling older, frailer. There had also been a snapshot of a woman with bright red hair, wearing hot purple trimmed in electric blue. She had snapping green eyes and was grinning gleefully, a martini glass raised in salute.

Mom! Taylor'd concluded, sure she was right.

The clothing in the dresser beside the bed was not old. Youthful, stylish, a traveling wardrobe in navies, grays, and whites with red accents. The jewelry she had on, a mixture of gold and silver, turquoise and diamonds pleased her. In a small pouch under a handful of silky panties she'd found a turquoise and silver necklace, old, antique maybe, and earrings to match.

We are expecting to do some fancy dressing at some point.

Foolish to travel with good jewelry.

He bought it for you and he likes to see you wear it.

You think?

Taylor's musings over the revelations of her search were interrupted by a decidedly Wild West sound, the mooing of cows and the rumble of large beasts in motion.

More like Texas than Switzerland.

She got to her feet to peer over the hedge that separated the garden from the road.

"Switzerland!"

It didn't say Switzerland in your passport.

Sometimes they don't stamp them until you leave and then only if you ask.

And you know this because?

There were a considerable number of cows thundering by, stirring up a cloud of dust, followed close by a thin teen who seemed to be urging them past the chateau, waving a green T-shirt and yelling in French and Italian.

"Hurry! Help!" Marta shouted to Taylor, running across the courtyard and down the drive.

Responding to the urgency in her voice Taylor dropped her book and joined the chase.

"The cows, they must not go across the tracks or into the fields," Marta called, flapping a tea towel in the face of a large bovine intent on turning into the drive.

The creature mooed plaintively, swung its big head away, and continued up the road toward the intersection. Marta scampered along the edge of the road surprising Taylor with her agility.

"Wave, yell," she called over her shoulder.

Taylor waved and yelled, wishing she too had a tea towel to defend herself from the herd of white and tan, brown eyed quadrupeds who didn't appear to be paying her efforts a great deal of attention.

"They must go down to the river," Marta shouted.

You're going to get yourself trampled.

"Shoo, shoo! Not so close!" Taylor swatted at the swaying sides of a cow that seemed inclined to run her off the road.

Did a cow run you into the ditch this morning?

The stampede, urged on by Marta's flapping tea towel seemed to stream off the left side of the road and out of sight. Running behind, slapping at the flanks of the last cows as the teen continued to flap his shirt, the three of them issuing encouragement in French, Italian, English, and Spanish, Taylor felt her heart begin to pound and remembered the pills in her purse.

Are you supposed to be doing this?

I speak Spanish.

So so Spanish.

You're panting.

Reaching the point where the cows left the road she found herself on a short rutted and churned up dirt lane that went off at an angle, ramping down to a wide flood plain along the river. The cows had slowed, some were beginning to munch, nose down into the knee high buffet of grass and wildflowers. Their forward motion was stopped altogether by a wire fence that ran down the hill from the road and into the water parallel to the railroad bridge high overhead. Parallel with the other side of the bridge a second fence enclosed the space under the span and beyond that was a long, and from a cow's point of view Taylor guessed, even more lush expanse of grass.

"Bien, merci," the boy gasped.

"The cows used to graze there," Marta pointed to the greener grass on the other side of the fences, "But the dairyman's uncle who owned it died and he left it to his son who keeps goats there now. The cows are not really allowed here, but they sometimes get out. If they aren't caught they can do damage in the fields."

"They like zucchini?"

"The young plants, and they like the grapes. Marc would lose his job if they got into the fields and he needs it," Marta said softly, nodding at the boy who was hunkered down in the middle of the rutted lane catching his breath. "The owner of the cows will come and they will drive them back later. Thank you for helping."

"It certainly was exciting for a minute there."

Taylor noted her heart had stopped racing and her breath was coming easily.

So, I'm not a total invalid.

They'd been walking up the lane and Taylor turned to scan over the now calm, almost bucolic, scene.

"I can see why the cows were so intent on getting there," she said looking back to the long expanse the other side of the trestle.

"Yes," Marta agreed.

They stood watching the swiftly moving river, the grazing cows, and the clumps of flowers bending and bobbing as the wind ruffled the grass. Then a bit of brown, a log, Taylor thought at first, caught her eye as it bumped downstream and caught in the first fence where it went into the river. The "log" twisted in the current, pulled sideways around the post and into the no-cows land under the bridge.

"It's a body!" Taylor whispered urgently, grasping at Marta's arm with one hand and pointing with the other.

CHAPTER 4

The authorities had come and gone. Marta'd translated Taylor's description of what she'd seen, which wasn't much. Taylor'd been kind of disappointed they'd asked so few questions.

It wasn't the crime scene.
The body just floated in from upstream.
What did you expect?
More.
Morbid curiosity is... well... morbid.
If you want to solve a mystery, find out who you are.
Give it time, you'll remember.
What if I don't?
You will.
Listen to the optimist, a snide voice snickered.
Better than listening to the cynic.
A little healthy cynicism is a good thing.

"Taylor?" Marta said softly, rousing her from her introspective.

"Mhuh?"

Taylor looked up from the book that lay unopened on her lap. She noticed the shadows on the garden path had grown considerably.

"There is a call for you."

"Me?" Taylor asked startled. "Who?..."

She accepted the cream colored cordless receiver Marta extended.

Hello?"

"Hello darling," it was Chris, she recognized his voice. "Our meeting's gone rather long so we won't be back for dinner. Please tell Elsbeth we're sorry. Maybe we can get together later in the week."

"I... Who?..."

Taylor searched in vain for any memory of an Elsbeth.

"Marta will explain. We may be late so don't wait up."

"OK," she said, feeling confused.

"Taylor, I love you. If you don't remember that, you will. Just be patient now, you'll remember everything eventually. Got to go."

The line went dead and Taylor was left clutching the phone to her ear wishing for some voice to explain who she was, who Chris was, how this gorgeous, charming man came to be her husband. Suddenly, like a cold wind swirling through her foggy memory she remembered clearly not believing him. Remembered at one time being very sure he had hidden motives behind his words of caring adoration. What she couldn't remember was if she'd been right.

"It is not necessary to change for dinner. Elsbeth is very casual," Marta said, taking the receiver as Taylor slowly lowered it. "We will walk. It's not far and it's supposed to be pleasant tonight. A jacket would be good for coming home later."

Taylor nodded still twisting the certainty of distrust for Chris's words that roiled within her. She went up to the room, combed her hair, checked her makeup, sighing at the bruises, and took a navy jacket from the armoire. At first her idea was to stick a lipstick and comb in one of the big pockets but instead she picked up the denim tote and slung it over her shoulder.

Always need your pills with you.

Right.

Another thing remembered.

Taylor stopped at the bathroom on her way down.

Always go before you leave the house, Mother used to say that.

Everybody's mother says that.

Smile, Taylor ordered herself seeing her grim face in the mirror. She smiled, running her hands through her hair to give it some height. Then she shook her head and watched the tiny silver and turquoise earrings - mini versions of the ones wrapped in tissue and hidden under the panties - twinkle. Her smile broadened, warmed, and felt real.

Always smile, another thing mother used to say. It will make you feel more confident, and people will wonder what you're smiling about. No one wants to know why you're frowning.

Mother was right.

Feeling lighter, even a little amused at her predicament, Taylor exited the bathroom. She found Marta waiting for her on the porch, the only difference from the brown slacks, long sleeved white blouse and sturdy brown shoes she'd been wearing earlier, a paisley jacket in shades of brown, cream, and navy.

Elsbeth it turned out was Marta's sister and she lived less than a mile away in an apartment.

"They had a lovely home in Bellinzona but, several years ago now, there was a terrible car accident. Her husband and son were both killed instantly. She was in the hospital a long time and was unable to face going back to the house. A mental breakdown the doctors said," Marta shook her head, frowning. "She was grieving. But the doctors said it was a depression and sent her to the sanatorium. It took almost a year but eventually she was fine. Unfortunately, here in Switzerland, once you have been "ill" someone, a male member of your family, must sign. Take responsibility for you. Edward, our eldest brother, signed for her release."

Marta sighed as if to shift some heavy weight.

"So now she lives here in a tiny apartment with no garden. One day..."

They had walked to the corner, gone right, away from the river, and then, several blocks on, turned left. Marta paused before a stucco, three-story building, pale green and very plain with the same metal roll down shudders Taylor'd seen on the house in the vineyard.

29

"I have dinner with her every Tuesday. She makes all the old things from when we were children and we laugh about old times. Tonight she has promised me Priest Choker."

Marta smiled at Taylor's raised eyebrows.

"I will let Elsbeth explain."

Today is Tuesday.

The doctor did say he'd be back Thursday — in two days.

Priest choker?!!

Better not let the doctors lock you up here.

Priest Choker it turned out was coarse ground corn meal toasted in a cast iron skillet with finely chopped potatoes added toward the end. While Elsbeth stirred constantly to keep dinner from burning Marta told the story.

"Long ago, many people were very poor but very proud. It was expected to take one's turn providing dinner for the local priest. One family was so poor that when the priest came to them all that was in the kitchen was corn meal, a few potatoes, and milk from the goats. It was a meal often eaten by the family. But the priest was new to the area and very hungry. After blessing the food he dug in before they could explain how to eat it. He choked and died."

Elsbeth served them each a steaming bowl. At each place sat a second bowl and a soupspoon. Marta brought a large pitcher of milk from the refrigerator and filled the second bowls.

"See," Elsbeth demonstrated, "you take a spoonful and dip it in the milk, to keep from choking on the cornmeal."

Elsbeth and Marta watched anxiously while Taylor followed directions.

"But that's good," Taylor said after the first bite. "Are there onions in it too, I didn't see you add any."

"No," Elsbeth explained, "It's the toasting, the carmelization of the cornmeal and the potatoes that gives it the sweet vegetable flavor. And I always serve it with cow's milk the way our mother did."

"We had it often when we went to the mountain in the summer," Marta said. "I guess it was a hard time for mother but we children loved it. The trip up walking behind the cows, picking sweet grasses for the barn, the berries and the cherries gleaned along the way."

"The high pasture, so steep mother was forever calling us back from the edge," Elsbeth interrupted. "Just mother and the cows and sometimes a neighbor with goats and long, long summer days. I think it remembers better than it was. Are you sure you like it, Taylor? I can fix you some soup."

"Really, I like it. When I was small, my mother made a lot of toasted cheese sandwiches. Cheese was cheap, you could get a loaf of sandwich sliced bread for a quarter, I suppose that's why we had them so often, but it's still one of my favorites."

You remembered something!

Grilled cheese sandwiches, big deal.

"We have treacle for dessert," Elsbeth said. "A rich man's dessert to make up for a poor man's meal."

As they ate Marta and Elsbeth kept Taylor amused with tales of childhood summers in the Alps and the antics of their brothers and sisters.

"Naturally, I was always a very good child," Elsbeth said, with an impish grin that stripped off the years and exposed the bright eyed, pretty child she had been.

She set the glass bowl that showed off the layers of fruit, custard, jam, whipped cream, and sponge cake that made up dessert, on the table.

"Oh yes," Marta laughed. "A spoilt baby is more like it. She was the youngest and everyone spoiled her. She was always able to convince Edward to carry her. Remember; the brown cow loaded with big bags of flour and cornmeal and pots and pans. Edward held on to its tail to help pull him up the path with papa's backpack and you atop his shoulders. Mother was always in front with the spotted cow piled with bedding, Adie at the back to make sure none of us missed any good grass or lagged behind. And all of us singing, what a funny parade we made."

"The Von Trapps we weren't," Elsbeth said, laughing.

"But a close family," Taylor observed.

"Then, yes, we were. Mother kept us in line," Marta said and sighed and looked at her sister. "Now... If mother were alive Edward wouldn't even think of forcing you to give up your share of the chateau."

"If mother were alive she would be a hundred plus, and Edward would be trying to talk her out of the whole place," Elsbeth said, banging her dessert spoon on the table. "For years the place wasn't good enough for him. He hated it the whole time we were growing up. At first we only owned the big room," she explained to Taylor. "The one with the new kitchen and a part of one bedroom upstairs. It took papa over fifty years, almost until he died, to own it all. He paid dearly for the last piece, old William's storeroom."

"I don't understand?" Taylor said.

"The Swiss traditionally don't like to borrow, or lend. So over the centuries they've bartered," Marta explained. "If a man needed a bit of land no matter how small to pasture a goat or a cow he bought it, or, more likely, traded another bit of land, or space in his house or barn. Real ownership, an exchange of title. When the Italian Count whose grandfather built the chateau fell upon bad times — some stories say he was a gambler, others that his family lost favor in Italy — either way he ended up in debt and the chateau was split up to satisfy that debt. And divided again many times over the centuries. Papa told me once the records showed as many as forty different owners at one point in the late seventeen hundreds. There must have been at least a dozen when we first moved in."

"A kind of condominium," Taylor said.

"Sort of," Elsbeth agreed. "Edward was embarrassed because we were poor. When he was 17 he went off to the German part of Switzerland. He worked for a cabinetmaker and went to school. Eventually he came back here, started his own business, did very well, married, and built a fancy house. Every few years his house is not good enough for him and he builds a new one. Bigger and better. Jeanine, his wife, is a good woman, but she doesn't stop him. Now it is popular – prestigious – to own an old chateau, particularly one you can say has been in the family for a long time. He wants us to sign papers promising we will leave our parts of the chateau to him."

"When you die you mean?" Taylor asked. "But didn't you say he's older than you?"

"I don't think Edward thinks he is ever going to die," Marta said with a grimace. "As long as Adie is alive he leaves me alone. But he is always after Elsbeth, hinting that anytime he wants he can withdraw his sponsorship and have her returned to the sanatorium and just take her part as his due."

"That's awful," Taylor said. "Isn't there anything you can do?"

"Behave myself," Elsbeth replied. "Just sit here in my little apartment and tend my knitting." She laughed. "Quite literally. I knit several hours each day. I take some special orders and do sweaters and caps I sell to one of the shops in town. I even made Edward a sweater last Christmas."

"I think she should have stuck him with the needles," Marta said.

"Talk like that is exactly what could get me in trouble," Elsbeth cautioned, looking around as if Edward had suddenly appeared in the room. "He makes a report of everything to the doctors and makes it all look so bad. When I wanted to go to the mountains for the summer when I was first released – we, my husband and I, owned, still own, a house, a barn we converted, up high with a great view and cool in the hot weather — Edward convinced the board that can recommit me that I was suicidal. He told them he was afraid being alone in a place where I had had happy times would depress me. I asked about it every year in the beginning, now I don't bring up the subject."

Elsbeth blinked, her face gone emotionless, her thoughts lost behind unseeing eyes.

"Edward hints heavily that if she would sign over her share of the chateau now it would demonstrate reasonable thought. He doesn't see why she wants it anyway. Says it would be foolish for her to spend money converting the rooms above Adie's into an apartment. And since he controls her funds it will never happen."

"Unless I outlive him," Elsbeth said, animation returning to her face. "The old goat can't live forever."

Taylor had finished her treacle, and wondered if she wanted more. She had been so fascinated by the sisters' tale she didn't remember what the sweet tasted like.

Do I have a weight problem?

Don't remember any diets.

Well that's convenient.

"Yes, please," Taylor answered as Marta finished serving herself some more and offered the bowl to Taylor. "Adie, you've mentioned her several times. Is she away or..."

"Adie seldom comes out of her rooms," Marta interrupted. "A neighbor, Gretchen who is the daughter of the man who owns the cows, is with her on Tuesdays when I come here."

"Edward would like Marta to help him convince Adie to move to elder care," Elsbeth giggled. "Last time he mentioned it to Adie she told him off good and he didn't visit again for almost six months. Adie is the oldest, none of us could ever get away with a thing with her. After mama died she even kept papa in line."

"And it was Adie who arranged to lease part of the west wing," Marta said. "The income from Piet's studio makes life a lot easier. Adie never married, I was widowed a long time ago and my husband was not rich. Elsbeth is the one who married well."

"Much good it does me now," Elsbeth sighed. "Willhelm's family is gone, his father, mother, and only brother all of influenza many years ago, when Wilhelm was still at university. Now there is only an old cousin, in Geneva, who sends me sweet letters once a month. Edward will have even more money to keep from me eventually."

"You must feel angry, frustrated," Taylor said.

"Frustrated, yes. Angry? I suppose. Edward, I think, truly believes women are unable to make reasonable decisions for themselves. He feels he is taking care of me — he lets a lot of his personal desires color his decisions. But then there has never been a time when he was not trying to manipulate things to get what he wanted. It is who Edward is, and for all that he is a good man, a good father. It is his view on the world, despite his great vain desire to be fashionable, that is so behind the times, so much a relic of the very roots, the poverty, old ways, and lack of respect, he hated."

"That's our Edward, self-centered, hardheaded, bent on having his own way," Marta said with a chuckle. "But, still, at times totally lovable."

CHAPTER 5

They walked back to the chateau through the warm velvet of a starry night.

"The stars are bright because there are no street lights," Marta said, waving a hand over her head at the great expanse of the universe. "There are those, developers, young people who know no better, that wanted to put street lights on every corner. But there was a protest, hundreds went to the town meeting and for now the stars are our light."

The black blanket studded generously with twinkling far off suns fell to the tree tops ahead of them but was cut off short to the left and rear by the precipitous rise of the mountains. The town, Marta explained, was small, squeezed between the lake and the Alps.

"Lost in time some, like Edward, say. But if this is lost then I hope we are not found."

"But Edward stays here?" Taylor wondered aloud.

"He is a big frog in this little pond," Marta said lightly.

Headlights from behind cast their shadows, long and thin before them and they moved to the edge of the road to allow the vehicle room to pass. It suddenly occurred to Taylor that they were both wearing dark clothing and not easily seen. She stepped farther onto the grassy verge and felt the ground sloping off steeply into the drainage ditch.

Careful, one fall a day is more than enough.

It was a car!

A car from behind.

The black car?!

Don't jump to conclusions.

A black car. It was a black car.

Perhaps it was only the darkness, or perhaps there were just a lot of black cars in Switzerland, but Taylor was sure the car that passed them was a black car. The same black car she had seen that morning after her fall.

Duh, so the guy you saw leave earlier has come home.

But this time there was only the driver. No passengers in the back that she could see. No face - no familiar face - in the passenger seat.

I know who that man is.

Sure you do.

A neighbor you've met maybe.

Someone I know.

"We must ask Chris to speak to Edward about a picnic," Marta said. "Edward is impressed by your husband and will be eager to please, particularly if he has a chance to show off his forest project."

They moved back to the center of the road after the car passed. Ahead of them they watched its taillights turn left as they would themselves.

"Perhaps Lars and Laszlo will join us and we can parade up the mountainside to the high pasture as we did fifty years ago, Adie, Edward, Peter, Petra, baby Elsbeth, and I, following mother and the cows."

"Peter is your other brother?"

"Yes, married to a French woman. They live in Zurich."

"And Petra?"

"A sister."

There was an odd catch in Marta's voice.

"She is gone, disappeared, a long time ago. When I was seven, no eight, it was right after her thirteenth birthday."

"How terrible."

"It hardly seemed real. At first mama and papa were sure she was hiding, she was always pulling some prank. But after two or three days when everybody had looked everywhere the grownups began to whisper. I think they were sure that her body would be found. It never was."

Marta fell silent. They walked on, turning the corner and then turning again into the cobbled drive of the chateau without further conversation.

"The car is not back," Marta remarked as they approached the dark building where only a pale light shone through the first floor windows on either side of the big fireplace. She fumbled along the wall beside the deep-set door and with the click of one switch a light came on in the stairway and beside the door at the far end of the porch.

Taylor knew it was the entrance to Piet's studio. The knowledge was suddenly there like the light going on.

"Piet is a sculptor. He does some original work but mostly he makes copies for museums."

"You remembered!" Marta said, opening the big door. "Would you like some coffee? Surely they will not be much later returning."

"Coffee would be nice."

Taylor did not want to be alone just yet.

And when Chris gets back you will be alone with this man who says he is your husband.

Why would he lie?

Not like you're such a hot commodity.

Something is going on here, something secret.

Why are we here?

Who is the missing Laszlo?

Why did I get a flash of terror when I saw Lars?

Paranoia.

You were frightened by Santa Claus when you were three.

I was not.

The arguing voices in her mind both comforted and frightened Taylor. They were familiar and yet, she was certain, not normal.

Marta crossed the great room turning on lamps to cast soft glows across the furniture and created shadows on the stone walls. When she got to the kitchen, that part of the vast room burst into bright light. Marta flipped the switch on a thoroughly modern and rather intimidating looking coffeemaker.

"I need to check in with Adie and see that Gretchen gets home to her bed. Be right back."

Taylor'd paused inside the door searching the room for a memory that went back beyond this morning, the doctor and lunch. She walked slowly around the dining and sitting areas examining each chair, each picture, lamp, the very stones of the wall wanting them to speak to her. She was staring at her own reflection in the mirror when Marta returned.

"Taylor, you are all right?"

"Trying to decide if I looked familiar," Taylor said as lightly as she could manage. The aroma of the coffee wrapped her as she turned, she heard the bubbly hiss of the machine.

"Everything OK?"

"Adie is fine. I told her about the picnic. She wants to come, too."

"Come! I thought she was ill. Bedridden," Taylor burst out in surprise.

"Not ill. Tired. Bored with living. Ninety soon and not perhaps in the best shape for a trip up the mountain but I doubt we could convince her of that if she chooses to come."

"But you said you had a sitter, Gretchen, the cow owner's daughter?" Taylor said still confused.

"Adie teaches her how to make cheese, the way our mother used to. The way our grandmother and great-grandmother did, and about wine from the dandelions, and chicory in the coffee, and polenta, and honey from pine tips. Gretchen's mother is very modern, a nurse. Like Edward the old ways have never interested her. Gretchen is still a student. The university gives special credit for documenting the old skills. Like oral histories only more exact about the doing — recipes, methods. They would talk all night if I let them."

"Has Elsbeth fixed her priest choker?"

"Edward does not approve of Elsbeth having company," Marta stated flatly. "He allows our Tuesdays because Adie and I insisted it would be good for her," Marta poured two tiny cups of the black, pungent, and piping hot liquid she called coffee.

"Will it cause a problem then, my going with you tonight?"

"Not at all since we are not going to tell him," Marta said with a little laugh.

"But she won't be able to come with us on the picnic?"

"Edward is not the only manipulator in the family," Marta put the cups on a tray, added a small pitcher of cream, and brought it to the table.

CHAPTER 6

The sound of voices roused her from a shallow sleep. She had lain awake for some time willing herself to remember her husband, her children, life before she woke up in the drainage ditch, and failed miserably. Sleep crept over her unwelcome, casting her into a dream world peopled with strangers in strange locals. For a second or two the room around her was another such site, foreign and foreboding like the inside of the pyramid her dream self had just been wandering through.

"But why would he have gone without telling us?" said a deep voice in the hall. "Laszlo has always been a bit of a loner but what possible separate agenda could he have here?"

"None. I would bet my life on it. He's been kidnapped, or lured away with no time to tell us he was going," a familiar voice said.

Chris! It was comforting to recognize his voice with such certainty.

The thought reassured her almost as much as the words she'd heard distressed her. Taylor rolled onto her back and her inner counsel exploded with views and opinions.

Kidnapped!

What kind of a mess has Chris gotten you into?

It's not Chris's mess.

What makes you so sure?

"Best get some sleep," Chris said, "We'll have to come up with an excuse for his absence in the morning. I don't want them getting nervous about our intentions at this point."

"I agree," the low voice replied and Taylor surmised it was Lars. "Sleep well."

"You, too," Chris said.

Taylor heard Chris enter the room. She'd intended to ask him flat out what was going on but suddenly she was shy and pretended to be asleep. In what seemed seconds she felt the side of the bed sag under his weight, her pulse rate sped up and panic threatened to overcome her.

You don't know who this man is.

My husband, he's not going to hurt me.

And you know that how?

What's all the secrets and whispering about?

Who are they trying to convince of what?

You should ask him to sleep in the other bed!

Taylor opened her mouth but before she could speak she felt his body shift and extend next to her. His presence alarmed her but she did not want him to go away.

We're married.

Hump, some disbelieving prude within huffed.

"Taylor. Taylor, wake up. The doctor said I was to wake you."

"Umhuh," Taylor mumbled.

"Are you OK?"

"Uhhuh," she lay still somewhere between comforted and scared stiff, the scared stiff side getting high points when she felt his arm slide across her possessively.

His hand closed on her midriff under her right breast, and she felt a soft kiss on her cheek then, nearly at once, she heard his soft breathing and knew he was asleep.

Well!

Disappointed?!

I am not!

What were you expecting, the man said he had to get some sleep?

I wasn't expecting anything.

Sure.

I wasn't.

Go to sleep, there aren't going to be any answers tonight.

Her sleep was uneasy. Lars' face loomed large as she clung desperately to she knew not what and feared for her life. A dark handsome man, not Chris, held her close and

42

laughed down into her eyes. Black sedans raced back and forth across a zucchini field as she pedaled furiously on a bicycle that did not seem to move. She swam through great blue green waves chasing Chris and felt angry and exasperated when at last the sea spewed her out in the middle of a jungle in front of an angry looking man in pajamas. Chris and Taylor danced in moonlight on the warm sand, and Taylor sat in a large leather chair at a big desk and watched a city fade in the distance while great stacks of paper were sucked out the window. Each time the panic roused by the dream threatened to wake her she would become aware of the warm presence of the arm that pinned her to Chris's side and feel safe, slipping back into her haunted-house dream ride.

There was a golden shaft of light angled low through the tiny window at the back of the room gilding the air and teasing Taylor into wakefulness. She lay still at first enjoying the warmth of the bed, pretending not to notice the hand cupped possessively around her breast and the steady breathing of the large man to her left. She snuck a peek in his direction.

He even looks good in his sleep!

She regarded him for several minutes, studying the even features, the sandy brown hair, resisting the unbidden urge to lean across and kiss the gently parted lips. Taylor sidled carefully from beneath the possessive arm and tiptoed toward the window, pulling a comforter from the end of the second bed to wrap around her against the chill of the morning.

At first she saw only trees and rooftops and the mountains - vertical granite giants skirted in green, their gray heads lost in the clouds - rising behind the town. Motion off to the left caught her eye and pulled her back to the near neighborhood. Across the tangled back gardens of the chateau, in the lane, the one they had strolled last night to Elsbeth's, Taylor saw Marta, walking swiftly, a basket over her arm. She passed out of sight behind some trees and houses only to reappear in seconds hurrying back toward the chateau, her basket bobbling.

Well, I'm not the only one up.
She'll have coffee made.
Shower. You need a shower.
Right.

A course of action set, and agreed upon, Taylor tiptoed back across the room, quietly gathered clothing and her tote and slipped out the door. There was no sign of life, she noted, in the unlit parlor at the far end of the balcony. With quick steps Taylor turned the other way and rushed down the cold stone stairs ruing her failure to look under the bed for slippers.

She showered and dressed in gray knit slacks, a soft white turtleneck, with cuddly white hooded cardigan to ward off the morning chill and the same white leather sneakers as yesterday. Taylor carefully hung her wet towel, fluffed her short damp hair, then checked her makeup wondering if it was more or less than what she usually wore. She had used a lot of eye shadow to balance the purple/green tinge. Taylor rolled her pajamas into a ball and stuffed them in the bottom of her tote thinking to return then to the room later.

Don't want to wake him.
Coward.
Got that right.

She'd also been right about the coffee. The aroma engulfed her when she opened the door. The table was set for breakfast. The outline of two loaves of bread under a bright white cloth topped a cutting board in the center of the table surrounded by dishes of butter, jars of jam, and pots of honey. In addition, under a bell glass there was a small board with a large wedge of a pale soft cheese.

"Good morning," Marta called from the kitchen. "We are having a Swiss breakfast today. But you may have eggs, too, if you wish, or perhaps porridge?"

"The Swiss breakfast sounds perfect, if I can have some coffee right away," Taylor answered wondering what a Swiss breakfast entailed.

The promise of coffee pulled her across the room to the dividing counter.

"Certainly," Marta said, turning to fill a cup.

Taylor wanted to ask her what the bit in the road was all about. Everyone seemed to have secrets.

Perhaps it is Marta you should distrust!

Don't be silly.

Why should you distrust anyone?

What was she doing out in the middle of the street in the wee hours of the morning?

Ask her.

I will.

None of your business, no need to be rude.

I'll find a nice way...

"Oh, this is wonderful," Taylor said, taking a sip of the strong, hot brew to which she had added the merest drip of cream. "I will be quite spoiled by the time we go home."

"Thought I'd find you here," Chris said from the door. His hair was still damp from the shower, the dark suit he wore positively GQ.

Expensive!

Not how I remember him.

You don't remember him.

Apparently not.

How'd he get dressed so fast?

"I didn't mean to wake you," Taylor apologized.

"I always know when you're not there," Chris said, smiling down at her. He accepted coffee from Marta with a nod of thanks.

"How's the memory?"

"Still among the missing. Did you find your friend?"

You know the answer to that.

45

But I don't know if I'm one of the people he wants to make excuses to.

"No, we didn't, and not a hint of a possibility. I'm worried. We'll have to proceed without him and hope for a break of some kind."

Proceed with what?

"Marta, I hate to impose," Chris continued. "But since Laszlo isn't available to support Lars this afternoon..."

"I will make you a trade," Marta interjected. "I will take Taylor to lunch with my friend Nita in the city if you will talk to Edward about a picnic Saturday. I thought Taylor would enjoy a visit to the new forest and a trip up to the summer meadow."

"Hey, I don't need a babysitter!" Taylor protested.

"I was only thinking that after your fall you shouldn't be alone. We'd planned to take the airfoil across the lake to Italy for some shopping but we'll have to do that another time. Before we go home. I promise."

Chris smiled, fixing her with his blue eyes, and the majority of Taylor's righteous indignation faded.

"But Marta doesn't have to spoil her lunch plans," she said. "I'll be fine here alone. I've got my book, it's beautiful in the garden."

"We can stop at the market and pick out the meats for the picnic. And maybe visit Tante Renee. She'll feed us little cakes and French chocolate."

"Well, if only for the sake of the little cakes and French chocolate," Taylor said, giving in gracefully.

"I smell coffee," Lars boomed coming through the door. "And I'm hungry."

"As if that were something new," Chris chuckled.

"There are two loaves of bread, cheese and cured meats to get you started. And the last of last summer's berry preserves to fill in the cracks," Marta told him crossing from the kitchen with a platter of what looked to Taylor like exotic deli meats. "Would you like eggs, too?"

"No, no. A good Scandinavian breakfast is just fine," Lars said, taking his seat.

"Swiss," Marta corrected. "Your mother fed you griddle cakes and sweet rolls and fat sizzling sausages."

"Ah but my grandmother spoiled me with gammon and smoked sausage and...," Lars had cut a thick slice of bread, spread it generously with the creamy cheese and topped it off with several paper thin slices of a meat that looked like uncooked Canadian bacon, his sentence was cut short by the taking of an immense bite but his praise was continued in the rolling of eyes.

"We share a great-great-grandmother," Marta explained. "His great-grandmother ran away with a merchant and it took three generations for the family to forgive her."

She returned to the kitchen for a thermal carafe.

"Coffee," she explained.

Taylor watched in amazement as Chris popped a tightly rolled piece of uncooked bacon in his mouth.

"Cured, like ham," Lars assured her taking three of the little rolls onto his plate. "One of my favorites."

"It is all your favorite," Marta teased, seating herself.

Taylor cut a slightly less hardy piece of bread than Lars or Chris, added cheese and a slice of what looked to her like summer sausage and with the first bite decided it was her favorite kind of breakfast, too.

But then you always liked cold pizza for breakfast.

I did! That's right, I do.

And bacon sandwiches.

Roast Chicken.

Anything Mexican.

Corn on the cob.

A whole list of favorite foods flooded back to her and she munched contentedly pleased to know a little more about herself.

47

A loaf plus of bread later breakfast was over and Chris and Lars had been thoroughly primed on what to ask of Edward. Taylor helped remove the dirty dishes.

"We shouldn't be so late tonight. Last night we wanted to put out some feelers... about Laszlo." Chris caught her to him as she turned back from the counter for the rest of the plates.

"Emh ahh?... er," was all she could manage, full of questions but not knowing how to put them.

Chris noted the puzzlement in her eyes and kissed her heartily.

"You'll remember eventually, darling. I refuse to believe I am all that forgettable. See you for dinner."

He kissed her again, prolonging it. When he let loose and turned to go Taylor felt bereft.

A girl could get used to that!

Apparently you did once.

Yeah!

Careful!

She followed him to the door and waved, watching them drive off in still another black sedan.

A rental.

Was the sedan that hit me a rental car?

"I was hit, I was trying to get off the road and the black sedan hit the handlebars," Taylor said to the morning in general.

CHAPTER 7

The trip to the "city" as Marta had termed it was a short train ride. They walked to the station, seven longish blocks that took them away from the zucchini fields and scattered houses, past the long driveway of the dairy and into the cobbled streets of some past century. An illusion spoiled almost at once by the large sign over the door next to the pastaria, Internet Café it proclaimed in half a dozen languages including English. At the end of the block the street veered left, to the right was a roofed rail station platform.

"Like Disneyland," Taylor said, charmed.

I've been to Disneyland!

With the children.

And their names are?

Hell if I know.

Taylor frowned, disturbed to be unable to name her own children but pleasant, smiling faces swam in her head and she relaxed knowing for a fact that all was right with them.

Disneyland was a long time ago.

"Where do we get our tickets?" she asked.

"We pay on the train."

Minutes later a picturesque green locomotive that would have done Disneyland proud chugged into the station and, along with a small crowd that had appeared from nowhere, they swarmed into the bus-like interiors of the passenger cars. As Taylor mounted the steps she saw, farther along the platform, a quick exchange of canvas bags and the tossing off of several packages expertly caught by a short man in a tight green uniform.

"Give the conductor two euro dollars," Marta instructed, pulling a like amount from her own black leather wallet.

There was a double high-pitched whistle followed by a long blast and the little train chugged on. The twin of the uniformed man on the platform bustled down the aisle, people noted their destinations and passed over their fare. He repeated the various names of towns and stations and made change with quick hands, nodding at the end of each transaction before moving on.

They picked up speed and Taylor was enchanted to find they were moving along a river.

"Will we cross our bridge? The one across from the chateau?" Taylor asked.

"That is behind us. We are going the other way. Three bridges and we are there." Marta told her.

They wound back and forth across the river passing green fields – not zucchini – pastures with cows and sheep, and small, two-story stone huts.

"Barns," Marta explained. "Old ones. Many were torn down and the stone reused. Now they are protected, even the ones past repair. Heritage some say. To keep us picturesque and please the tourists, Edward claims. It is popular to remodel them into little houses. You will see our barns in the high meadow. The cows lived below and we above."

As they came off the third bridge there was a flash of rooftops then the train entered a rail yard, sliding as it did so between two giant freight trains headed in the opposite direction. Marta gathered her purse and jacket in preparation. The train angled sharply left, past the end of one of the freights and across three sets of tracks, coming to a smooth stop at a covered station only slightly larger than the one they had embarked from. Taylor followed Marta off the train into a milling crowd.

Keep up.
Don't get lost.
You don't know the language.
You don't know anyone here.
You don't know who you are, let alone anyone else.
Oh, for Pete's sake, you are not a child.

Taylor clutched her tote to her, trying to feel the hard outline of the tiny bottle of pills among the other contents.

Breathe! A stern inner voice commanded.

This is just a pleasant trip to lunch.

Relax and enjoy.

"Right," Taylor said, obeying the order.

"What?" Marta asked stopping at the curb of a busy intersection where cars and trucks whizzed past at dizzying speeds.

"Nothing," Taylor said, noticing that there were an awful lot of black sedans on the streets. "How far to Nita's?"

"She lives at the far end of the park. You can see the trees where the street angles," Marta said, pointing across the intersection.

Sure enough, about three city blocks up the wide street with a double set of trolley rails up its middle, Taylor could see a mass of green foliage on the left, and below it grass and masses of red flowers. Taylor watched a red trolley jog suddenly to the right and disappear.

"Now," Marta said, stepping off the curb and making haste across the street as cars and buses came to impatient halts.

Taylor hesitated long enough to be sure the traffic really had stopped then followed.

"How many people live here?" Taylor asked, reaching the far curb.

"Nearly thirty thousand," Marta told her proudly.

Thirty thousand! There were more than that in my neighborhood in Chicago.

So now you know you lived in Chicago.

I knew that yesterday.

Grew up there.

"Lots of banks," Taylor noted as they passed down the block.

Every second or third window displayed exchange rates and/or stock quotes.

"This is Switzerland," Marta replied.

They paused, along with a half-dozen others, at the next intersection. This time Taylor both saw and heard the signal to cross as, with the tinny brrring of a cheap doorbell, a mechanical arm lifted on a post on the far side of the street and ordered, she imagined, walk. Two blocks later, traversing the length of the park, she was reminded again of Disneyland.

Clean.

As if someone had just swept it.

Not a weed in sight.

They crossed a street and entered a six-story stone building with an unpronounceable name - at least to Taylor - over the door and the date 1812.

"No elevator," Marta apologized. "But we go only to the fourth floor.

Lunch was delicious, a kind of kabob with pork, chicken, and two kinds of sausage served with a green salad and hot rolls. Talk was of family and friends who Taylor wouldn't have remembered just now, even if she had known them. She attempted to keep an interested smile on her face as her mind wandered.

Black cars that knock people off bikes and don't stop.

Maybe they didn't see you.

Maybe.

Black cars that have familiar looking passengers.

Why are you so sure you knew that man?

You don't even know your own husband.

That's another thing. Husbands that look too good to be true.

And you know what they say about things too good to be true.

And Laszlo, the missing man.

And dead bodies.

You didn't tell Chris about the body.

Not your body to worry about.

Trust.
Who?
Why?
What does Mr. Too-good-to-be-true do for a living?
Who was Marta meeting on the street this morning?
Don't get all upset until you're sure there is something to get upset about.

The internal discussion heated up as pessimist, optimist, pragmatist, paranoid, and practical peacemaker vied for dominate place. Taylor could feel her heart rate increase. Stubborn practicality won out and she settled back to enjoy the fruit and cheese that ended the meal.

Chocolate and little cakes at Tante Renee's gave Taylor time for another interior battle. Tante Renee, who looked, Taylor was sure, like her own grandmother, if only she could remember what she looked like, had company, friends who spoke only French and German. Renee spoke only French, Marta Italian and French plus English of course, and Nita Italian, German with some English. Not one of them spoke Spanish and Taylor was sure that was the only language besides English she came even close to speaking. The conversation whirled about her with stories being translated, repeated, and translated again. Everybody talked at once, and though Marta and Nita tried to keep her in the loop, so much had to do with people and times Taylor didn't know that her counsel of selves claimed her attention with their own eddy of observations and speculation. It was warm in the little parlor, too many people in a tiny room, the chocolate and little cakes delicious but far too sweet. Battered by the babble without and the brouhaha within Taylor started to feel lightheaded. The pessimist pushed the panic button and it took great effort on the part of practicality for her to slow her breathing and maintain until at last the visit was over and they were out in the sunshine walking toward the station.

Taylor gulped the crisp air and, determined to put a stop to all speculation, forced herself to window shop. All the harder to accomplish when so many windows were devoted to Euros versus the dollar or yen. Over the top of one such set of quotes, running in digital lights along the bottom of the window, she spied him.

The man from the car! Their eyes met and the man quickly turned away.

He didn't recognize you.

Did too.

He was surprised.

He was angry.

Afraid.

He didn't want you to see him.

It wasn't him.

Then Taylor and Marta were past the window and she was staring at white soccer shirts with broad blue stripes and feeling foolish.

You can't even remember the face of your mother - how can you possibly remember the face of a man you saw for mere seconds in a passing car?

They turned off the block before the train station and shortly entered a large square, ringed on three sides with buildings whose graceful arched facades spoke of other centuries. The fourth side screamed today, if not tomorrow, in steel and glass.

The long case of meats in the deli held most of the familiar and ten times that in exotic and unknown. Taylor was tempted to ask for one of everything. She was particularly fascinated by the wide selection of pressed meats.

"Chipped beef?" Taylor asked pointing at tissue thin slices of prime rib as another memory flooded back. "Do you have to soak it?"

"Soak it?" Marta asked bemused. "It is tender, like the best steak."

"To get the salt out," Taylor said.

"Salt? But it is not salted. There is some that is peppered."

In the end Marta selected two kinds of pressed beef and several types of thinly sliced sausage including one that looked like it was made of gristle and another that appeared to be a checkerboard of white fat and pink baloney. At a bakery they bought several dozen cookies, very short and full of nuts.

By the time they arrived back at the station, Taylor had the day's exchange rates memorized and drawn the conclusion that there were nearly as many shops selling Benneton sportswear as banks in Switzerland. The thick white cotton knit shirts with the one broad strip (mostly blue) and matching collar were everywhere. Three of the passengers on the train wore them.

CHAPTER 8

The train ride was short, the walk back to the chateau long with their load of packages, and Taylor was glad when at last they entered the dark cool of the great room.

"After I put everything away we shall have some lemonade and cookies," Marta said. "But first I will tell Adie we have returned."

"I can see that for myself."

Adie was both taller and thinner than Marta. Silver hair, also thinner than Marta's, cut in a similar short cap curled beguilingly around a face that was pretty despite the obvious signs of age. She was wearing a collarless dress printed with tiny lavender flowers and shoes that, Taylor found, struck a chord.

The eighties. My daughter wore them. Black lace-up oxfords with a two-and-a-half-inch chunky heel.

You told her they were like the ones your great-grandmother wore.

Sturdy and sensible, Great Gram called them.

Hot, was your daughter's term.

What's your daughter's name?

Never mind, I remember my great-grandmother.

A frail woman with a steel will. Dark taffy hair, barely gray at the temples, done up in braids that wound around her head like a halo. Taylor remembered pound cake and homemade jam and green tea. She smiled.

Adie smiled back, her bright, dark eyes cracked with laughter at her sister's surprise.

Marta, mouth open, stared without speaking.

"Edward is coming for dinner, to discuss the picnic," Adie said. "I thought he might find it easier to accept my joining the party Saturday if he didn't find me hiding in my rooms like an invalid."

"And he won't argue in front of company," Marta said, with a positive nod.

"That, too," Adie agreed. "Taylor, there is lemonade, but also you could have a Campari cooler."

"The cooler sounds just right," Taylor said.

"Good."

Adie whirled into action and Marta busied herself putting away their purchases.

"Tonight we shall have polenta, made as my mother made it," Adie said as she filled glasses with ice. "And liver with onions. Do you like liver?"

"Yes, I do," Taylor said, knowing in that instant that she did. "But my children hated it."

They were sitting in the garden sipping the frosty drinks when Chris and Lars returned.

"So," Adie said, ignoring Lars' raised eyebrows, "Have you found your misplaced friend?"

"No, and it is most unlike Laszlo to go so long without checking in, at least a note or..." Lars shook his head grimly. "He is the one who coordinated this particular project from the very beginning. I fear..."

"That he is going to miss the picnic completely," Chris finished lightly.

"Ah, but that will mean more for the rest of us," Lars said, all seriousness gone from his voice.

It was a quiet evening. Taylor was amazed to watch Adie sit, almost in the fireplace among the glowing embers, stirring constantly the large pot to which she'd added only course cornmeal and water. In the kitchen Marta, in obedience to Adie's firm directions, tended the rest of the meal Adie had set to cooking before she settled in to stir the polenta.

"It was easier in a way," Adie said, "when all the pots were in the fireplace."

When the simple mush began to thicken, great bubbles bursting like lava, spitting hot motes, and the stirring more and more of an effort, Marta brought the rest of the food to the table including the ever-present bread and cheese. Lastly Marta sat a thick and ancient looking board perhaps two feet square slightly hollowed from long use, in the center of the table.

"It is ready, Edward," Adie said, lifting the wooden paddle from the pot and moving aside. Edward knew his part and with oven mitts to protect his hands lifted the large pot, turned to the table, and quickly poured the thick mixture out where it stood steaming, a good three or four inches proud of the board.

"Mother used to do it with just her apron to protect her hands," Adie remarked, her face was flushed with the heat and exertion. "Marta, show Taylor and Chris how to serve themselves."

Marta plopped a large spoonful of the hot mush on her plate and then topped it with a slice of the cheese, topping them both with another plop of mush.

"Like a sandwich," Marta explained.

She added two ladles of the slivered liver and onions in a dark, herb flecked tomato sauce to one side.

"While it's hot," she encouraged.

While they ate Edward told them of the mistakes he thought the man who'd bought his business was making. Taylor waited for him to protest Adie's and Elsbeth's plans to join them Saturday for the trip up into the Alps. He spoke of his son and his hopes he would not marry the latest girlfriend.

"She is French, like Peter's wife, I can wait for grandchildren until he finds a nice Italian girl."

He grumbled of being busier than ever since his retirement.

"My wife has projects for me, my son has projects for me, the government has projects for me. And then there is Elsbeth," Edward rolled his eyes.

Marta opened her mouth, and then, catching sight of the slight negative shake of Adie's head, shut it again.

Taylor wondered why Edward's wife wasn't present but decided it was not a politic question. Chris and Lars kept Edward talking about himself, avoiding any reference to Laszlo or what their business in Switzerland entailed.

"Saturday morning at eight-thirty, sharp, here, ready to go, tell Elsbeth. It will take us half an hour to get to the forest and at least until noon to get up the mountain. Some of us are not so young as we once were," Edward said when he was at the door.

"Your arthritis is bothering you again?" Adie asked sweetly.

"Not so much now as in the winter," Edward said flatly. "How are your knees?"

"No pain at all," Adie told him with a smile.

"We," Lars said, including Chris with a wave of his hand, "have to spend a couple of days in Geneva. But we'll be back Friday night. We will be ready."

"Saturday morning then," Edward said and left.

"You lied," Marta said with a giggle as soon as the door was shut behind him.

"Not really a lie," Adie said with a shrug. "I have no pain as long as I take my medicine. If he can walk up the mountain, so can I."

Adie and Marta excused themselves to the kitchen to clean up.

Lars poured another glass of the Merlot Edward brought, and excused himself as well.

"I have some reading to do to be ready for tomorrow. Today they drowned us in paper, none of it in English of course. I will make you translations of anything important," he said to Chris.

He lifted his glass in salute and left them alone.

Chris switched off the light over the table leaving only the one lamp on the sideboard. There was a glow from the fading embers in the fireplace. Taylor felt suddenly shy and went to stand before the stone hearth, her glass in hand.

"A long day," Chris said from close behind her. He slipped his free hand around her waist.

"Not so bad," Taylor said. "I remembered my great-grandmother and what foods I like and..." he kissed the nape of her neck and she remembered that she liked that, too.

Careful, the paranoid shouted.

You like it, go for it, the optimist pushed.

But...

Before any more opinions could be voiced, Chris had nibbled first an ear and then the corner of her mouth.

Unwise! Unwise! Was shouted from some dark corner of her mind but Chris claimed her lips with serious intent and all discussion was tabled.

"I promised you this would be a romantic vacation with only a little business," Chris said, using teasing kisses to keep her from speaking or objecting. "How about we take our wine for a nice walk in the garden and then..."

"About that little business," Taylor said, trying to regain some emotional equilibrium. "What, exactly, are we talking about?"

"You don't remember then?" Chris asked.

His arm was still about her waist and he moved her toward the door.

"You know the doctor did say it was best for you to reach recall on your own."

It was cool outside, nicely so after the warmth of the fire and the wine.

"You don't do something illegal do you?" Taylor asked, only half teasing.

"No," Chris laughed. "I'm one of the good guys. You can trust me."

"I get the feeling, well... that maybe I didn't always trust you," Taylor said, stopping in the deep shadows of the rose covered garden shed.

She looked up at his tall form, back lit by the lights on the porch and the balcony above.

"In the beginning we didn't trust each other. But we worked that out."

He took her glass from her and set both of them on a table. Then Chris gathered her close.

"I love you Mrs. Robbins, loved you from the minute I first saw you even when everything I knew said it was a bad idea. You'll remember, and I'll wait till you do."

His head came down and she lifted hers without thinking.

We certainly fit.

Does he call this waiting?

Oh shut up and enjoy.

"Ohh!" Taylor said, when at last she got a chance to take a breath. "That was very familiar.. nice. I mean, I think I remember feeling like that. But then I'm old enough to have been kissed before and to have felt like that, you know, how it feels when you're really kissed and... it might not even have been you I remember... kissing me, that is. But it was very nice, the way I felt... and familiar, like I said, and would you please shut me up, I'm babbling."

"You do that sometimes," Chris said gently and kissed her again.

Taylor considered telling him about seeing the man from the car in the bank, but it seemed silly and unimportant.

Even if it was the same man, what difference does it make?

Standing there in the dark garden, the night air infused with the scents of lavender and roses, the clear sky sparkling with stars, warm, arms holding her against a broad chest where a heart thumped solidly in her ear, so what if she saw the neighbor at the bank.

"Mmmmhuh," she said, and yawned.

"You need a good night's sleep," Chris said. "And I need to see how Lars is doing with those translations."

CHAPTER 9

Taylor pedaled as fast as she could down the rows of the zucchini field to keep ahead of the stampeding cows. Santa Claus popped up from behind a giant hummock of squash and she changed course to avoid him, bumping across the road and into the vineyard where the long tendrils spiraled around her ankles and the spokes of the bike, holding her immobile as the cows thundered toward her.

"Shush, it's all right darling. Only a bad dream."

Taylor felt a strong arm pull her closer and relaxed to walk on warm sandy beaches.

Again the early light slanted across the room to wake her. Curiosity tugged Taylor to the window. She twisted the metal haft and pushed, it opened easily. The morning air was sweet, scented with an ancient flowering vine that twined its way up the side of the chateau and climbed diagonally across the body of the building. Its far end draped luxuriously around the rusted iron balustrades of a balcony on the third floor of the wing to her right.

A balcony fit for a Juliet.

As long as her Romeo is an accomplished stunt man.

Somewhere in the nearby trees a bird was greeting the morning with gusto. Taylor looked left just in time to see Marta returning from the same direction as the day before.

Uh-oh!

Ask her, there's probably a very simple answer.

Don't ask too many questions - could be the missing Laszlo asked too many questions.

You have entirely too much imagination.

Taylor pulled her Levi's and a navy hooded T-shirt from the dresser drawer along with some undies, scooped up her tote and leather sneakers and, with a last look at the sleeping figure of her husband, one arm already searching for her missing form, made for the stairs.

Showered, dressed, and ready for the day she exited the bathroom to find Chris leaning comfortably against the wall near the stairs. A blue silk robe tied loosely at the waist, sockless feet in shiny loafers, his morning beard gave him a macho look that balanced the little boy grin on his face.

"I thought about joining you, but..."

"The door was locked," Taylor said, alarmed and pleased at the same time.

Chris picked up his shaving kit and suit bag from the steps, "Coffee's ready. The aroma hit me like a fist when Lars opened the door."

Entering the main room, Taylor found the coffee ready and breakfast laid out for three with Lars already smearing apricot jam on a thick slice of bread.

"No Marta?" she asked.

"Dentist appointment," Lars said between bites. "She brought in the bread and ran for the train."

"I swear this bread still feels warm. Does she bake every morning?" Taylor cut a slab from the crusty loaf.

"No," Lars laughed, a fork impaled a roll of his favorite bacon half way to his mouth. "When I said brought in the bread I meant from the bakery cart. He still delivers every morning as they have for decades. Once with a pushcart, now it's a van. He stops at each intersection on his route and all the women come from their houses."

"Oh!" Taylor said and remembered now that Marta had explained just that the first morning, the day before her bicycle ride.

So much for that little intrigue.

"Lars, when we met before, was it Christmas?" Taylor asked, filling her cup from the carafe.

"Yes. You remember," he said, nodding.

"Sort of. I keep thinking of you in a Santa Claus suit." She stirred cream into the dark steamy liquid.

"I wear it once, for a couple of hours at the party."
He cut another thick slice from the loaf, slathered it with
butter, added a slab of cheese, and topped that with a
spoonful of jam. "My wife will put me on rice cakes when
I get home but for now I eat," he said and took a big bite.

"Your wife spoils you shamefully," Chris said,
coming through the door. "She will fix you waffles and
sausage…"

"And put the rice cakes on the table and look sad if I
reach for seconds of anything else," Lars said, laughing
between words.

When breakfast was over Chris and Lars drove off in
their black sedan and Taylor dared to take the dirty dishes
as far as the sink. She covered the bread with the white
cloth as she'd seen Marta do and set the glass bell over the
cheese. The small platter of breakfast meats had been
emptied. Taylor poured herself the last of the coffee and
went outside to sit on the wooden bench that stretched
along the porch toward the entrance of the studio. The
doctor would come at ten, Marta was due to be back by
noon — it was only eight. Adie, she supposed, was in her
apartment but Taylor felt shy about disturbing her.

You are a big, grown up girl, amuse yourself.

Taylor went to peer through the studio doors. The
walls were a glossy white hung with large black and white
photos of what she assumed to be Piet's sculpture framed
in bright primary colors. There was a massive modern
desk with a computer and pale yellow chairs for clients she
supposed near the door, and on the far side of the room a
sitting area comprised of white leather couches and
hammered metal tables in front of a black marble fronted
fireplace. By pressing her face against the glass she could
just see the work area toward the back where several large
sheet covered shapes looked like a gathering of snowmen.

Or ghosts!

Taylor wiped at the smudge of makeup left behind on the otherwise print free glass.

"Won't take a Sherlock Holmes to figure out you snooped," Taylor mumbled.

She took her empty cup back to the kitchen and started back to her room to put away her pajamas and get a sweater, the intent being a nice walk, maybe to the intersection where Marta picked up the morning bread.

As she slid the folded night garments under her pillow a dull thud and a drift of fine dust from the ceiling brought her erect.

Adie, downstairs?

But she could still see a fine powder drifting from between the boards above her, glinting momentarily as they passed through the slant of sun from the window, then landing almost invisible on the floor and coverlet. Taylor listened, breath held. At first there was no more sounds but the source of dust shifted, toward the window, angled toward the stone wall behind the bed. Then there was a scraping.

Something heavy being dragged?

None of your business.

Your imagination.

This is a bad idea.

Taylor pulled the gray zip-front sweatshirt from the armoire and put it on, awkwardly switching her tote from hand to hand, on her way out the door. In seconds she was in the narrow passage that led to the floor above. She noted a narrow, rounded door set in the stone wall on the right but did not slow to examine it. The stairs were unlit and each step upward the gloom deepened. Ten steps up another small, arched door led off a wide landing but it was locked. The stairs turned, not as she expected them to over the lower staircase, but at a right angle into the core of the house. Taylor continued up, heart pounding, adrenaline flowing, searching in her tote as she went for the small penlight she had seen there Tuesday when she'd been looking for hints of her identity.

Lipstick.

Mascara.

"Aha!" She switched it on and let the thin beam play up the steps into the blackness. There were footprints in the dust, large ones. "Lars, looking for Laszlo," she told herself aloud and was surprised by the slight echoing.

There was a pattern of circles in the print and she tried to remember if Lars' shoes were rubber soled. The prints, despite the easy explanation, brought a tightening to her stomach, the light flashing across the stone steps and walls inspired a chill of fear.

Memories?

But not good ones!

Foolishness.

Foolishness is climbing into other peoples' attics looking for scary stuff.

"It's not an attic, it's the third floor. I'm exploring. Nobody said not to," she said, moving forward.

At the top of the flight Taylor emerged into the remnants of a long past world. Left and right there were great gaping holes in the floor, her sweeping light exposed broken and missing boards. A pile of stone rubble and a couple of steps to nowhere suggested that once the stairway had continued upward, perhaps to the roof. There was a bit of planking, some newer — less, perhaps, than a hundred years as opposed to five hundred plus — that led off to the right.

"Left is over Adie's rooms," she said in tour guide fashion running the beam over the pit where far below wires and metal conduits criss-crossed the floor and signs of reinforcement and repairs could be seen. On the right both splintered planks and rubble littered the floor of what Taylor surmised was the room behind the arched door. She ran the light along the newer planks that crossed an expanse of collapsed floor next to a flaking plastered wall. Taylor paused to admire the faded fresco of a slender brown-haired woman with a water jug, the surface of the painting so cracked it seemed to be made of worn pieces of jigsaw puzzle.

"Bet you've seen a thing or two over the centuries."

And kept them all to herself.

The planks continued right, into the dark.

Go back down. Now!

Footprints go that way.

Thud must have come from over there, too.

Floor must be good, no big holes in your ceiling.

Doesn't mean it can support your weight.

If it supported Lars it can take me.

How do you know it was Lars left the prints?

Despite the plethora of good advice Taylor was advancing slowly but surely on what she took to be the safest route along the three board wide path whose paler color and finished edges spoke of having been milled sometime in the last century.

You are one stubborn woman.

The thought cheered Taylor immensely. She knew it was so and the idea pleased her.

"I am a doer, not a watcher," she told the darkness about her.

Vertical slits of light indicated the position of the boarded up third floor balcony and a pie slice of a hole let in a beam of sun.

There could be bats in here!

And mice.

Rats! There could be rats!

Now you think of it.

And the bats...

Or the rats...

Could have caused the thud.

Taylor had advanced far enough to find solid looking flooring extending in all directions. Wooden partitions loomed out of the depth of the darkness leaning at odd angles. She followed the footprints as they slew left.

The bedroom should be about here.

Farther on.

There is only one set of prints, going and coming.

Lars would have noticed, no one else has been up here in quite a while.

Right!

Uh oh.

The thought had been made a lie. On her right all kinds of shoe soles had come and gone, layered until it was impossible for her to tell how many and in what order. A bit of light, like the flame of a candle from a chink in the flooring, almost at the middle of the well-trod area caught her eye and she knelt to peer down into her bedroom.

"Well!"

But what did they hope to see?

A voyeur?

Pretty dull, watching people sleep.

People, married people, do sometimes do something besides sleep you know.

Then why in the middle of the morning after we'd gone down to breakfast?

To see if the room was empty.

A thief?

Taylor swung her beam in rings around the mass of footprints until she found a path of overlaid prints headed to the backside of the chateau. She spotted parts of the circle pattern and knew that Lars, if it were he, had come this way too. In the corner, almost to the back wall there was an open doorway, a short passage through the stone encased in great thick posts and beams that led in a half dozen steps to a space that looked very atticky indeed.

Cables and conduits cut across the floor in random pattern. The light from an unshuttered half round at the top of a window cast a dim glow to show additional partitioned off spaces.

"And this is the space over Marta's apartment where Lars and the missing Laszlo are staying."

There was a rustling in a dark corner and Taylor froze.

Bats!

Dummy, bats would be on the ceiling.

Rats?!!

Either way her stomach was churning and she had to remind herself to breathe.

A pair of yellow eyes approached out of the darkness. Taylor quit breathing all together and watched mesmerized as what had at first seemed the world's largest, blackest rat stalked toward her from the shadows and morphed into a fat black cat.

"Hello there," she said, exhaling. "Guess you wouldn't allow bats or rats would you. At least not the four-legged kind."

Taylor was answered with a polite meow and then her host or hostess led the way off to the left along a stone wall to another small arched door. This one was ajar, and askew, one iron hinge having come loose. It was a small room, a dozen feet square at most, with one very dirty set of French doors that allowed spotty patches of sun to pool on the floor. The cat stretched and then lay down. Taylor stepped around the door and chuckled.

"You must be Juliet. I was admiring your balcony this morning. And I'll bet you were chasing about making a bit of noise earlier. Did you catch breakfast?"

"Juliet" meowed and cocked her head at an angle.

Taylor could see no prints on the floor. A dark wood paneled wainscot ran around the room head high topped with a narrow shelf broken only by the door, the window onto the balcony and a small fireplace at the right end whose tile face had been pried free leaving broken bits behind.

"You have a lovely parlor."

Taylor crossed the room to assure herself this was the balcony she'd seen from her bedroom window. The French doors, she found, had been nailed shut.

To keep Romeo out?

But squinting through the dirty panes of ancient flawed glass she could see the back wall of the chateau and the tiny windows that dotted its vast stone expanse. She could also see that Adie's end of the building had more and larger windows and a sunlit patio, filled with pots of flowers, and separated from the tangle of the back garden by a vine covered wall.

"I wouldn't want to leave all this for a retirement home either. Tell me, Juliet, what other guests have you had recently?"

Juliet yawned.

Taylor considered looking for another access to this floor but then remembered the doctor was due to arrive soon.

"So nice to meet you, do try to keep the noise level down will you," she said to the cat and headed back the way she came.

She was in the timbered passage when she heard the same scraping noise as earlier and paused. Seconds later Juliet let out a loud elongated meow and streaked by headed toward the stairway. Taylor turned her light back toward the gloom of Marta's attic. There was nothing, only silence, then from below she heard Adie calling.

CHAPTER 10

You didn't want to keep Adie and the doctor waiting.
You didn't hurry that much.
You were scared witless.

Taylor rinsed the soap and the last of the third floor grime off her hands, grimaced at the purple and green tinged side of her face, and turned off the water.

In the great room Adie had served the doctor coffee and cookies and they were chatting in Italian.

"I was upstairs, the third floor," she confessed. "The fresco looks very old. Oh, and I met the cat, she's a darling, does she have a name?"

"The cat," Adie said with surprise. "I don't think Marta ever named it. One of the electricians who wired Marta's apartment left him to reduce the rodent population, which he does admirably."

Not Juliet but Julius it would seem.

"So, tell me, Mrs. Robbins. You have remembered what happened and all about yourself?" the doctor asked.

"Some, sort of," Taylor said, accepting a cup of coffee from Adie. "But there are still huge blank spaces, bits of memories or feelings that don't fit together."

"It will all fit, as you say, soon. Rest, enjoy Adie and Marta's fine cooking and by the time your bruises have faded your memory will have cleared. But, here, sit, let me check your eyes."

Taylor put her cup down and submitted to his gentle exam.

"It is as I said, in a day or two you will no longer be so colorful and your blank spaces will be filled. Have you had any headache?"

"Not really, just a little the first day."

"Bien, very good. Then I shall have another cup of Adie's excellent coffee if I may and perhaps another of the little pastries and then I will go to see old uncle Niccoli's gouty toe."

It was after lunch, while Marta and Adie were doing the dishes and Taylor had been banished to the garden to read, that she saw the black sedan again. It careened around the corner, spitting gravel and sped on toward the other chateau. Taylor rose and climbed atop the garden table to watch it disappear in a cloud of dust that suddenly dissipated at or near the other chateau. She was sure the car had turned in there.

Or zipped right by and is half-way to Zurich by now.

This is not the road to Zurich.

Geneva then, or Bellinzonia.

This is not the road to anywhere.

There are only more fields of zucchini and more vineyards that way, Marta said so.

When you rode off on the bike.

You remember!

Yes and the names of my children and my grandchildren, too.

And that Chris used to be a policeman but now he writes books and gives lectures.

Pleased with herself she returned to her book.

It was a quiet afternoon. Taylor held a basket while Marta picked chicory and arugula and endive for a salad and told Marta about her adventure on the third floor.

"Julius. A good name for him. I was told not to make a pet of the cat, only to put water out, so he would feed himself. Which he does, there is much less scurrying above than once there was," Marta said standing erect to place a carefully selected handful of burnished arugula leaves in the basket. "Father always kept a dog but Adie never liked cleaning up after them and didn't want another after the last one died. The cat has very clean habits and the traps did not work well. Piet complained they made more noise going off than the rats did and most of the time they were empty. He wanted to put poison everywhere but Adie and I were afraid for the birds. I am surprised you did not step on a trap up there, they are still everywhere and nasty things."

"Was it so bad, so much caved in, when you were children?"

"No, well... some, even then. As the stones fell and the floorboards cracked, people were happy to sell. Father always told mother he would make repairs when it was all his — by that time she was gone and he was too old to care. When we were young we would play in the empty rooms, hide and seek, ghost, children's make-believe games. There is one room — with a little balcony — we would play Rapunzel. Petra in particular, she would spend hours there, reading or just dreaming, hiding from her chores."

"That's the room Julius took me to. I think he likes to lie in the sun coming through the French doors."

"Father nailed the doors shut after Petra disappeared. He couldn't get it out of his mind that she had fallen from the balcony. He must have gone into the Bueler's vegetable patch — that's what the back garden was then — a dozen times looking for her body. Afraid he would find her, I think, and afraid of what else might have happened to her if she was not there."

By late afternoon Taylor had finished her book and took it up to exchange for one of the others she'd discovered at the bottom of the suitcase. It was while she was trying to get the suitcase to fit neatly back into the armoire that she spied several sheets of paper stuck in the molding behind Chris's neatly hung clothes.

He must have missed his briefcase with these.

Mr. Efficient isn't so perfect after all.

I was beginning to wonder, always dressed and ready, everything put away in the blink of an eye.

Give the man a break.

The top page was just a list of dates with dollar amounts — large dollar amounts — after them. The second page more of the same ending in a list of names, some paired with a combination of letters and numbers, like vehicle license plates. A good third of the names had no numbers, only a row of question marks. Taylor recognized some of the names and gasped.

"Terrorists," she said in a stage whisper and gulped, her heart beating a mile a minute.

Easy now.

So you've seen those names in the paper, big deal.

How do you know you're even remembering right?

Could be, must be, more than one man in the world with that name.

But three names, no four. Those four for sure.

Taylor's head spun.

Not a good set of names to be involved with no matter which side of the table one's on.

The third page was another list of "license plates" paired with dates but no names.

Chris said he was one of the good guys.

Well he has nasty, dangerous playfellows.

Indeed he does.

Chris was a good guy and he dealt with some very bad people. But that had been in the past, hadn't it?

What's going on now?

"Well, husband dear, we are certainly going to have to have a little chat about the things I remember, and the things I don't remember or don't know and should, when you get home."

CHAPTER 11

Dinner was light – roast chicken and salad plus the ever-present bread and cheese. There were baked pears for dessert. Taylor enjoyed every bite, found stories about her children and grandchildren came to her lips without effort, was even able to recant a childhood tale of her mother, one about tomato soup and grilled peanut butter sandwiches. As she did, a clear picture formed in her mind of her mother in leopard print spandex, jumbles of jewelry and fire engine red hair boarding a plane, one of a herd of faux zebra, tiger, giraffe and panda – or perhaps it was skunk – clad octogenarians off to the ends of the earth bound and determined not to let any single senior discount go unused. Taylor smiled, she remembered her mother. She remembered the wild, sometimes inappropriate, and often sexually implicit souvenirs she sent from the four-corners of the world. She remembered her penchant for blue gin, the Lindy, sea cruises, and bright red lipstick. And she remembered she had had a happy, if a bit unorthodox childhood where she'd been encouraged to set goals that made her reach, sometimes felt embarrassed, and always felt loved.

"Emmhuh? What? I'm sorry. Guess I'm tired," Taylor said, realizing she'd been asked a question. "I was remembering some more."

"I was asking if you wanted some more coffee," Marta said.

"No, thank you. I think I'll go to bed and read, maybe get to sleep early. I want to be rested and ready for our trip up an Alp Saturday and I seem to be an early riser."

As it was she didn't read long, replay of the events of the day invaded her mind and shut out the pleasant malice of the cozy in her hand. Reminded of the chink in the floor with a bird's eye view of her bed she searched the ceiling seeking it out, chilled at the idea that someone could be looking back.

If you'd remembered sooner you could have done a bit of bump and grind putting on your 'jammas.

If I'd remembered sooner I'd have changed in the bathroom.

Prude.

So, if you're so worried, why didn't you put a board over it?

If I can cover it up they can uncover it.

She located a dark knothole, decided that was the offending aperture and stared, heart pounding.

"Oh, for Pete sakes," she sighed, exasperated with herself, and turned off the light.

Some hours later she was roused from sleep by the familiar scraping sound. Grateful at first to leave behind an uneasy dream of endless search through stone corridors, the small thuds and scuffling overhead made her uneasy.

Rats.

Big rats!

Julius chasing rats.

There was a particularly loud thunk followed by what Taylor's active imagination quickly conceived as an expletive.

A rat stubbing his toe?

Yeah. A two-legged rat.

Don't be silly, it was Julius.

Cats don't thunk.

Or swear.

They do when they're catching mice.

Rats.

All right, rats.

Mice, rats, or even bats, Julius is on duty.

It could have been a growl.

The thought didn't help much. Taylor clutched the blankets to her chin and wished for the weight of Chris's arm, the warm maleness of him in the bed next to her. Memories of other Chrisless nights flooded back enforcing her sense of loneliness and confirming just how much she loved the man. Then other memories, times when Chris had been very present indeed, filled her head and soothed her anxiety, there were no more sounds from above and she drifted back into pleasant dreams of dancing in his arms on the sand, on cobbled streets and tiled plazas, and smooth wooden floors.

Not a beam of sunshine, but the low rumble of thunder heralded the morning. Taylor lay in bed and listened to the timpanic concert fade slowly off across the mountains that rose so steeply behind the little town. When it had quieted to a distant grumble she got up.

"Good, you are right on time," Marta said, setting the coffee carafe on the table. "I have fixed us fried mush. It is one of my favorites but there was not enough for Chris and Lars too."

When the plate was set before her Taylor recognized the left over polenta, sliced half an inch thick and fried a crisp golden brown.

"There is jam and apricot syrup but my favorite is the pine honey," Marta said, picking up a small blue and white ceramic pitcher from its matching saucer.

"Pine honey?" Taylor asked, following Marta's example and buttering the golden slabs on her plate as she waited her turn with the honey.

"It is illegal now, but some still make it. From their own trees and being very careful not to pick all the tips," Marta explained. "If you pick the tender new growth, when it is pink and full of nectar, and cook it down, you get a syrup. Dark, sweet, and sticky like honey."

Mmmmhuh," Taylor agreed with her first bite. "But why illegal?"

"People would come from the town, the cities, and pick, in the forests and the yards. Some even made it in great batches and sold it to tourists. The trees were not growing, not setting seed, you know, forming pinecones. Homeowners felt invaded, their gardens damaged. So, they made it illegal to pick the tips or sell the honey. This was a gift from a friend who harvests her own pines very carefully."

"Delicious," Taylor said, finding the dark "honey" intensely sweet and thinking she preferred it when bees played middleman in the process. "I go to get my boots and pants for the picnic after breakfast. You would like to see my apartment?" Marta asked.

"Yes, please."

"Good. We will check to see that Julius has water." Marta laughed. "Now that the cat has a name he becomes a pet. I hope he remembers to keep after the rats."

Marta's living room was all greens and cream, overstuffed, chintz covered sofa and chairs with lots of pillows and obviously loved and cared for antique pieces of various parentage. The kitchen filled the back wall of the living room, a tiny reproduction of the one in the great room complete with the dividing island. A hall divided the back half of the big square that was the chateau's south end, one door on the left led into the smallish guestroom.

"Laszlo's," Marta said.

Except for two pairs of black shoes set neatly, toes together next to the massive armoire and the masculine piece of black leather luggage on the bench at the bed's foot, the room looked unoccupied. The wall behind the bed and the adjoining window wall were of stone, the other two walls matched the wood panels Taylor had seen elsewhere in the chateau but these were painted a rich cream. The green and cream satin striped spread was tidy, a pair of matching decorative pillows neatly if a bit squarely in place. The brown leather wing chair and ottoman, with a pale green throw over one arm and a parchment shaded reading light hung to best illuminate the occupant's material looked inviting. The pair of tall windows opened inward to reveal a wrought iron fence — a mock balcony — and a view over the tangled back garden to the trees, neighboring rooftops and the gray green wall that was the Alps.

When Marta opened a similar window at the end of the hall, Taylor could see it had a real balcony, square with a metal ladder running perpendicular up each end to the floor above.

"See," Marta said. "A fire escape. The building code, when I got the permits to do my remodel, required a second exit. The ladder to the third floor," she rattled the ladder on her right, "is fixed but the other one stays up unless it is released and slid down from here."

"But how do you get water to the cat?"

"Oh, that," Marta said smiling. Across the hall from Laszlo's room were three doors. "See," she pointed to the door nearest the living room, "My bedroom, and next the bathroom and here," she flung open the near door, "the laundry room and the stairs to..."

"The attic. I mean the third floor."

It was a large laundry room, the two windows letting in lots of light. In addition to the washer and a dryer on the far wall there was an ironing board, a soaking sink, a line of cupboards with counter space to fold and shelves above and, something Taylor hadn't seen in years, a mangle. But what interested her most were the stone stairs that rose beside, twisted, and crossed above the washer and dryer, then twisted again out of sight into the ceiling.

At the top of the steps there was a door, a door with a dead bolt Taylor noticed when Marta opened it. Inside the door a blue bowl sat on a rubber welcome mat and held a small amount of water. Marta took the bowl down, rinsed and refilled it while Taylor gazed into the gloom of the third floor trying to see new footprints in the dust but unable to tell much except that she could discern the circle pattern of what she supposed to be Lars' shoes. There was no sign of Julius.

A quick peek at the bathroom and Taylor knew it was Marta who had designed the bath in the tower. It was a long rectangle, all white tile, chrome, with graceful porcelain fixtures lined along the left wall and dark green towels. The window at its far end fitted with a mosaic of green, red and frosted white glass.

"I like white bathrooms," Marta explained, as they continued down the hall. "Adie's is all beige and brown, and very pretty, but to me it feels dark. Her whole apartment is beige. Beige and white and browns, well, some lavender, too. It's quiet, she says, and calm. I guess I'm a little noisy. I put Lars' in here because I thought he might be less uncomfortable with it than a stranger."

Marta's big corner bedroom with two walls of windows was bright, airy, and very yellow. Yellow chintz in big and little prints covered bed, pillows, chaise, and windows. The walls and carpet were more of the rich cream. The dark wood of the four-poster, dresser, and night stand gleamed.

"It's beautiful," Taylor said, then giggled. "But... Lars... in that bed, with all those pillows."

"He didn't do too bad of a job making it," Marta said, tweaking a pillow into place. She went into the closet and returned with a hand full of clothes and a pair of sturdy canvas boots.

"Will I need boots tomorrow?" Taylor asked.

"No your little white athletic shoes will do fine. It is only that my ankles are old and tend to swell if I do not give them support on long walks."

They were passing Taylor's room when they heard a car below them on the drive.

"The police," Marta said, leaning through one of the stone arches to get a better view.

80

CHAPTER 12

This time the polite policeman had pictures both of the water soaked corpse and of a dark-haired, stocky man of middle years with intense eyes and grim countenance.

"You have never seen this man?" he asked as, side by side on the sofa, Marta and Taylor stared at the photos.

"Never," Marta said, shaking her head.

"Not until we saw him in the river," Taylor added.

"And you have not heard his name, Walter Altzen?" he asked.

"Not that I remember," Taylor said slowly as Marta again shook her head to the negative.

But you don't remember much.

Walter Altzen, think, you have heard it somewhere.

Oh, please, until a couple of hours ago you wouldn't have recognized your own mother's name.

"Did he live locally?" Marta asked. "Should I know him?"

"He was a tourist, according to his visa," he said and paused.

Taylor had the distinct feeling he had been about to say more and then thought better of it.

"Did he fall in the river, was it an accident?" she asked.

"We think not. According to the medical examiner his neck has been very deliberately broken."

Apologizing for the intrusion he refused the offer of coffee and left.

"Walter Altzen looked like a very unhappy man," Marta said as they watched the police car execute a tight three-point turn and depart.

"Somebody was certainly unhappy with him," Taylor noted and shivered as a cloud obscured the sun. "I hope it isn't rainy tomorrow. Think I'll go up and get a jacket."

Shrugging into her sweater she remembered why Walter Altzen's name had jangled a nerve. The name, or one like it, had been on the list she'd found in the closet.

"I'm sure of it," she said crossing to the armoire.

She'd put the papers back very carefully where she'd found them.

"There it is."

Almost at the bottom of the list, one of the ones with question marks instead of a code.

So what does it mean?

That Walter Altzen is a bad man.

And?

And his name is on the list because he...

Because he has done something Chris and Lars — and Laszlo — are concerned about.

Something that has to do with money and terrorists and...

Switzerland!

Wow!

That's why we're in Switzerland.

Chasing terrorists?

No... Chasing terrorist's money.

"Wait 'til I tell Chris."

He already knows.

Not about the dearly departed Walter Altzen.

Not that I remember who he is — what he does — what we are doing in Switzerland.

Does Marta know?

Taylor studied the three sheets of paper but could make no further sense of them and placed them back where she'd originally found them. She decided not to mention her great epiphany when she went back down. If Marta knew what Lars and Chris were here for then she didn't need to be told. And if Marta didn't know, then it wasn't her secret to tell.

Taylor curled up on the purple sofa, a warm throw across her legs, her book open on her lap, mostly for show, as she watched the leaping flames in the fireplace and analyzed what she now remembered about her life.

More.

But not all.

Not everything about the bike accident.

Not about Laszlo.

You don't know about Laszlo.

I do too.

You can't even remember his face.

Tall and dark and...

The man in the car and the bank?

Maybe...

See you don't remember him.

But if it was him, why? How?

Up through Marta's laundry room, across the third floor, and down the stairs.

Not unless he's the one with the circles on the soles of his shoes.

Those shoes went up and came down.

Or went down and came back up?

Well, that makes no sense at all.

Taylor made an attempt to move her thoughts back to happier memories: their condo in Mexico, friends...

Val, Dave and their children, Alice and Dill.

Good friends and business partners, too.

Val and Dave and Chris do lectures and teach classes to all kinds of policing forces.

Undercover spy stuff.

Right.

And sometimes they take a job.

Right.

And this is a job.

She was back to where she started. She began to read in an effort to divert her attention from the endless looping back and the frustration of not knowing what it was she wasn't remembering.

Chicken and the egg, a stubborn voice persisted in prolonging the interior argument.

Quiet!

CHAPTER 13

Chris and Lars didn't arrive until they were almost done with dinner.

"Sorry," Chris said coming through the door. "We had a bit of news we had to check out."

"There are some leftovers?" Lars asked with an appreciative sniff. "It smells wonderful and lunch was a very long time ago. This man does not consider the needs of others when he is busy at work."

"I wouldn't let him stop for pastries," Chris explained.

"Your supper is still warm, we have not yet had our dessert," Marta said, as she and Adie bustled about returning the just removed platters and serving bowls to the table.

"Ah, I was afraid that wonderful bouquet of pork chops was wishful thinking," Lars said, swooping in with a fork before the plate of crusty brown chops smothered in caramelized onions was settled.

"We can see that you have been wasting away," Taylor said with a laugh.

When dessert had been eaten and the next morning's plans discussed Marta and Adie washed up and Lars once more took a glass of wine and went off to do paper work. Taylor pulled Chris out into the garden despite the fine mist falling, anxious to tell him what she'd remembered and ask him a few questions about some things she didn't.

"Hey what's the rush, I want another glass of wine," Chris complained.

"Two is enough, and we have to talk."

"Oh?" he said, peering down at her in the faint glow from the porch lights.

"I've remembered some things. Lots of things but not everything yet. At least I don't think so."

"Such as?"

"That I love you like crazy for one," Taylor said, hugging him.

"I was counting on that. What else?"

"Why we're in Switzerland... I think. You, you and Lars and Laszlo are trying to find, to take or impound or some such thing, some money, from drugs, that belongs to a terrorist cell that has been funding suicide bombers and other equally nasty events in Russia. Right?"

"Right," Chris said and kissed her. "And I want you to note I told you all about it."

"Did you tell me all about Walter Altzen, too?" she asked.

Chris grinned, "They told us an officer had stopped by to see you this afternoon. No I didn't tell you about Altzen in particular because he was just a name on a list. I take it you found my missing pages. That's a relief, I was afraid we'd had a very sneaky visitor."

"We may have," Taylor said and told him about her visit to the third floor, the hole in their ceiling, and Julius.

"Julius may be the source of the noises, but he sure didn't make the footprints. Oh, darn, I forgot to ask Lars to see the bottoms of his shoes — I remembered about the storm and the prints on the stairs. Anyway, there is one set of prints, soles with circles on them, that goes up and down on the main staircase. The rest, well they could have been made anytime of course, but they come from the other end of the chateau. So they'd have to have gone through..."

"Marta's laundry room," Chris finished her sentence. "But I don't see how. They'd have to have come up the main steps, past our door to Marta's apartment, past Lars' door..."

"And Laszlo's door, or at least been across from it. Maybe he heard something and was kidnapped," Taylor speculated.

"Makes sense as far as it goes. The dearly departed Walter Altzen had his neck broken in a very singular way — right out of my text book — something Laszlo taught me. But I can't see them getting Laszlo out of the chateau without a struggle — noise of some kind. He had to have broken Altzen's neck before he was overpowered. How did we sleep through all that?"

"The stone walls?" Taylor ventured.

"You heard the cat."

"True," she snuggled closer, the light drizzle had begun to dampen her clothing and she felt chilled. "What do we do now?"

"We get you up to bed and warmed up."

"Oh," Taylor said not at all displeased with the idea.

What about Laszlo? her conscience demanded.

"What about Laszlo?" she asked.

"What little we could do has been done, the word is out. All that's left for us is to hope Walter Altzen's demise means Laszlo got away but has been unable to contact us. That, and to keep on with our negotiations with the banks and be watchful for some further attempt on the part of Altzen's friends to interfere. However," Chris was leading her up the steps to the second floor, "first we are going to get reacquainted."

"Mmmmm...," Taylor tightened her grip on his hand.

"And in the morning, early, you can introduce Lars and I to Julius."

"Should we cancel the picnic?"

"Absolutely not."

"Have we ever made love on a pool table?" Taylor asked lying in the warm curve of Chris's arm as the early morning light crept across the floor toward them.

"Almost. What made you think of that."

He rolled up on one elbow and looked down at her, his free hand caressing her hip.

"Just remembering. Speaking of which, aren't we due to make an early morning visit to Julius?"

Chris let out a sigh and threw back the covers.

"Go take your shower, I'll wake Lars."

Marta was just going for the bread when Taylor, Chris and Lars started up to the third floor.

"See, there are my footprints, where I go up and down," Lars pointed out. "And I check good because he could have come up the other way and then fallen in a hole," he waved the heavy duty flashlight he carried to illuminate the depths of the derelict second floor above Adie's rooms.

"Did you see the spy hole in our ceiling?" Taylor asked leading the way across the new boards, past the lady with the jug, toward the more solid expanse of flooring.

"Spy hole?" Lars questioned, his voice hushed as they entered the deeper gloom.

"Looks right down on our bed. Lots of footprints around it."

"Lots, I did not see lots of prints. Only a few, and old, like a curious worker had explored perhaps when they were putting in wiring for Marta."

"See," Taylor said as they played their lights over the floor above the bedroom.

"Lots is about right," Chris said, studying the patterns in the dust. "Someone came after your visit, Lars. And someone after you, too, darling." He held the light steady to show her small sneaker print half obliterated by a larger print with a waffle tread.

"Here is hole," Lars called, his big voice echoing in the vast empty space.

There was a skittering in the corner and Julius bolted from the shadows toward the timbered passage.

"Ooohho," Taylor moaned glad it was dark.

She was sure she was blushing.

Forgot the hole completely.

It was impossible to be sure exactly where waffle foot had trod in the mishmash of prints around the hole.

"No telling exactly when he was here," Chris said, guessing her concern, one arm coming around her waist to supply a comforting squeeze.

He may have missed the show.

"I think he knelt or sat down and got a good look," Lars said studying the marks on the floor.

Oh dear.

How embarrassing!

We are talking terrorist here, not voyeur.

A voyeuristic terrorist, the stubborn pessimist insisted.

"So, now what?" Taylor asked.

"Now we go eat our breakfast before the coffee gets cold," Chris said.

"Breakfast," Lars agreed.

"But..." Taylor said, following Chris as he turned back toward the stairs.

"And I think we should leave our sneaky friend a little something to peak his interest, maybe get him to expose himself," Chris said.

"A good idea," Lars agreed.

After breakfast Chris and Lars went up, "to get jackets" and returned just as Edward, and a man Taylor didn't know, with Elsbeth in the back seat, turned in the drive. Chris slipped his and Taylor's matching windbreakers into the trunk of the black rental sedan along with a blue knapsack almost hidden beneath the folds of Lars' voluminous blue jacket.

"Chris and Taylor, you come with me," Edward said standing in his open door. "David, will drive your car and follow with Lars' and the girls."

"The girls", Adie and Marta sniggled at the remark and seated themselves in the back of the rental.

David, Edward explained after they had loaded the backpacks with the lunch into the trunks, dispersed per his instructions, and were buckling their seat belts, was Edward's assistant with the forest project. "He is a student, he writes his final paper, his thesis you call it, on the old ways and the harm the land has come to."

"Harm?" Taylor asked.

"It's not really so much what you can see but what you can't see, and smell of course," Edward explained. "All the gleaning, the cutting of trees for firewood or just to create more pasture, turned the hills into grassy mounds. Lots of pasture, but not enough trees to keep the air clean, especially with the increase in people, industry, and cars. It had become a real problem. So the government set up a reforestation project, a volunteer program. Now we have replanted whole mountains. It is a young forest," he added. "But already there is a difference, they say."

They were soon speeding along narrow paved roads that hugged the winding banks of rushing waterways. Edward pointed out Roman bridges and new housing tracts. Elsbeth called their attention to picturesque houses; some of them fat, square, multistoried structures that once housed livestock on the lowest level with the extended family above.

"Apartments, now, many of them," she said, "even here in the country. Oh, and look," she pointed to a fairy tale castle of an edifice stretched elegantly along the banks of a tumbling creek. That is where we spent our honeymoon. Very romantic."

"Now Elsbeth," Edward cautioned solemnly.

"It is a happy memory, Edward. A very happy memory."

"It looks enchanting," Taylor said, admiring the turreted building with tall windows and dozens of cunning chimney pots adorning its steep roofs.

"We are almost there," Edward said, changing the subject. "We will park on the highway and walk up the lane."

In a few more minutes he'd pulled to the edge of the paved road, stopping in a wide spot where there was space for three or four more cars. "Where we parked our trucks," Edward explained. "The people on the lane did not want their road torn up."

Taylor agreed with them at once. The lane was time packed dirt, narrow, thick boughs of great ancient trees hung across it barely above Chris and Lars' heads. It led past a pair of stone cottages so small they would have fit together in the chateau's great room with space left over. Farther on, set back a bit from the lane was another house, another Hansel and Gretel cottage, with smoke curling out of its chimney and the aroma of fresh baking — something with cinnamon — wisping out to bedevil passersby.

"They have cut down the cherry tree," Adie lamented.

"It has been gone a dozen years," Edward said, pointing to the giant stump twined in yellow roses. "More. It has been a long time since you were this way."

"I suppose it has," Adie's chin went up and she drew her already squared shoulders back a bit farther.

She looked quite smart in brown twill pants and matching jacket over a red turtleneck sweater. She was, Taylor noted, still wearing the same sturdy lace up shoes with thick soles and clunky heel. Elsbeth and Marta both wore denim pants, chunky sweaters, and light boots. All three women walked effortlessly, matching stride with their brother. David, and Chris had the two large backpacks with lunch, Edward carried a canteen, while Lars sported the small blue knapsack.

In the beginning the going was flat, but at the end of the lane the already narrow road dwindled to an even narrower path between green pines whose wide prickly branches reached out to grab at one's hair and scratch at unprotected cheeks. The path, at first a gentle incline, was soon an outright ramp, a sudden turn around the base of a forest ancient let out into Edward's forest.

"Yiminie!" Lars exhaled.

"It's an orchard," Taylor said, remembering a long ago walk through an apple grove.

When was that?

A long time ago.

What difference does it make, I remember it.

Before them, climbing upward, beside them, lined down the slope they'd been ascending, acre upon acre of evenly spaced trees undulated on as far as the eye could see.

"Five kinds of trees," Edward said proudly. "The same as once grew here."

"But never so neatly," Adie said, with a chuckle.

Positively anal-retentive!

The thought leapt to mind from some smart-alec corner of her being and Taylor bit her lips to keep the words inside.

"We will be culling them randomly next spring," David said. "To make it look more natural. We expected to lose more to the weather but..."

"We did a good job, I got good stock. It is going to be a shame to cut any of them," Edward said, never slowing his pace.

He led them straight down a bowered row of ten to twelve-foot saplings to where the edge of the new forest met the random verge of evergreens that were the lower skirt of the mountain they would be scaling. Here they squeezed through a gap in a chicken wire fence — "to let people know this is the protected area" Edward told them — and at once the path changed.

Ever upward it wandered, zigzagging back and forth across the steep slope of the mountain.

"Step on the stones, not over them," Marta instructed Taylor. "They are fixed tight, like stairs."

"Cows went up stairs?" Taylor asked.

"Cows, and goats, and donkeys, even horses," Elsbeth said. "Oh, look, blueberries. But not ripe yet."

Beside the trail, the clump of bushes with dark round berries lured Marta to try one but she quickly spit it out.

92

"No, not yet. Too bad. Remember how we would pick it clean, and blackberries too, up a little higher."

"And the grass, it is so tall here. We would grab the handfuls, breaking it off so it could grow again, and we'd have a whole bag full to empty into the cow's feed box when we got to the top," Adie explained. "We carried bags, slung across one shoulder so they hung in front, sometimes two, one for berries one for grass. We were expected to fill them, even Marta, though I think she ate all her berries before we got to the hut."

"So did Petra," Marta said defensively.

"You ate your berries and most of mine," Edward said from the lead. "And twisted my ear if I didn't give you more."

The path got steeper, a literal staircase across steep stony slopes, through tiny wooded glades, between big boulders and, with the aid of stone slab or wood plank, over plunging rivulets. Taylor felt winded, her heart beating so hard in her chest she was sure they must all hear. None of the rest seemed to notice or be the least bothered by the climb. Crossing a sunny glade, the berry vines still in blossom, their stringers creeping out onto the path to snatch at shoe laces and pants bottoms, Taylor tripped, saving herself from a fall with a quick bit of footwork and the help of a convenient path side boulder.

"Hey, Edward. How about a rest stop," Chris called from the rear. "Lunch is getting heavy. You guys have had more practice at this."

They stopped there on the grassy, boulder-strewn slope in the shade of a gnarled spruce. David and Edward examined the scattering of small trees nearby. "They used to pull them, to let the sun in and keep the grass growing and the berries," David explained. "Here, left alone, the trees can replace themselves without our help."

"Our parents, like their parents and grandparents for hundreds of years, pushed back the forest, for food, for fuel, for survival," Adie said a bit defensively.

"And now, for survival, ours as well as the trees, we must help the forest return," Edward countered.

93

"Perhaps," Adie ceded with a sad smile.

"You doing OK?" Chris asked Taylor quietly. He'd come to stand behind the boulder she sat on, providing a backrest as well as a bit of a shoulder rub.

"I'll be fine. I can walk forever on the beach but, up hill... No one else seems the least out of breath. Not Lars or Adie or... I'm beginning to think I'm in worse shape than I've yet remembered."

"Your shape suits me just fine," he nuzzled her ear.

Taylor patted the black canvas tote, its broad straps pushed up over her shoulder so that it hung high under her arm. "And I've got my pills, I'll be fine. It's just making me feel foolish, getting out of breath so easy. Does this happen a lot?"

"Feeling foolish or getting out of breath?" Chris teased.

"Either, or," she said, leaning back more, feeling her own heart slow to match the steady beat in her ear.

"The out of breath thing is pretty usual," Chris told her. "It never seems to stop you, which, more than once, has been very foolish."

Taylor was just getting to feel caught up with herself when Edward rose and, followed by the others, trudged onward. A little over an hour and two more rest stops later they broke through a copse of young trees into a long meadow clinging to the side of the mountain like a porch roof wrapped around two sides of the house. At the eave end beyond a rambling and broken stone wall the grass dropped away, becoming a sheer wall of granite with trees and clumps of grass clinging in niches dotted across its face. Far below, Taylor saw a ribbon of green valley and a stream. Across the valley another mountain rose, and another, and another, each one higher, steeper, all of them looming so close that you had to put your head back as far as it would go to look up to the snow capped peaks. Up the grassy slope of the meadow there was a fringe of forest rising steeply into the mountain until the slope became so steep that there was only rock. About midway across the meadow there was a flatish spot, a short rise and then another flat spot on which two of the stone barns Taylor had become familiar with clung, as if they had been there for all of time. The heavy planks of the roof chinked with moss, the stairs up to the living space of the nearest one no more than sturdy poles sticking from the side of the building. When they reached the plateau she could see the second hut had a stone staircase.

"It never changes," Elsbeth said. "It has been thirty years, maybe more since I was here and it is still the same."

"No cow," Edward said.

"The goatherd's house is gone," Adie pointed off to a spot toward the edge where it appeared to be slightly stonier.

"Storm takes the roof and eventually nature reclaims it stone by stone," Edward said. "Hope you brought lots of lemonade, but first I want some water."

He took a tin cup from his pack and walked a few steps on to where water spewed from a cleft in a stony outcrop, like water from the kitchen tap. It fell into a shallow stone bowl and spilled from the bowl's lip to run across a gravelly bed between rocks in an arc toward the remnants of the goatherd's hut and the edge of the world. A thin stream, scant inches deep and less than a foot wide, it sang merrily as it sped on its way.

Adie was at Edward's heels.

"Cold and good," she pronounced taking a deep drink.

Soon the tin cups of icy water had been passed and Taylor had to agree.

"Such a little stream. But it never goes dry," Edward said proudly. "So little water, on hot days it almost evaporates before it hits the pool in the valley below. And in the winter it freezes to the mountain and makes a giant lip."

"We were not allowed to go past the wall, to the edge, but Petra wanted to see the water falling. She lay on one of the large rocks, right at the edge, right where the water falls and looked down," Elsbeth said. "She made me hold her feet, so the troll wouldn't get her. I was never so scared. It was supposed to be my turn next but mother caught us and switched our legs good."

"Troll?" Taylor and Chris asked as one.

"Mother always told them the troll who lived under the edge — or sometimes it was the ghost of children the troll had captured — would grab us if we got too close," Adie explained. "It was to keep us safe. I saw the waterfall once. Papa held me and told me to never tell mother. I was little, Edward was a baby. I don't think I've ever told anyone until now."

An amazing amount of food was pulled from the backpacks and spread on a blue blanket laid over the top of a great boulder poking its head up through the grass near where the stream spewed forth. Soon tin plates were piled with slabs of bread and cheese and deli meats, pasta salad, pickles and briny olives. Thermoses of lemonade and multiple refills from the cold, sweet stream washed down the feast. When Taylor was sure she could eat no more Marta rolled down the top of the baker bag on the shortbread cookies, all almonds, butter and powdered sugar with a bit of flour to keep them together. They melted in the mouth and filled in any chinks that might possibly be left.

"Now I'm supposed to be able to walk back to the car?" Lars lamented, taking the last cookie as he did.

"It's downhill," Edward said. "And nothing to carry. Not like when we had to carry the cheeses home, or wiggly little sisters."

"If we had any cornmeal or flour left Mother would trade it for cheese," Marta explained before Taylor could ask.

"It was a good plain cheese, hearty," Adie added, "And I think mother was sorry when the goatherd and his family stopped coming. They were company, especially when Papa didn't stay."

CHAPTER 14

The downhill trek took half the time of the uphill climb. Each tiny glade, each boulder skirted, each rest stop, passed now without a pause, evoked a sense of the familiar. It was an adventure Taylor knew she would welcome again. No wonder Adie, Edward, Elsbeth, and Marta had flown up the alp on the feet of their youth, aches and age swept away by the adrenaline of sweet memories. Taylor was sad to come at last to the orchard/forest and pass into the narrow lane.

"It's been a wonderful day. Thank you," Taylor told Edward.

"But it is not over yet," he replied. "We will take the long way home. You will see the snow and maybe the sheep. Then I shall show you a truly old village, like they used to be, and we will have dinner, if they are open, in a restaurant where David's second cousin's husband cooks."

After lunch Taylor'd been sure she would need no dinner but they'd walked about the meadow then down the mountain. Dinner, after snow and sheep and a little sightseeing, seemed an excellent idea. So it was — after feeling the sharp cold of a true alpine valley where the snow still lay thick in the mountain's shadow, and a glimpse of the people shy sheep with their great curled horns, leaping casually from one perilous perch to the next — that she found herself standing in the dark hush of a centuries old church.

They'd stopped to confirm the restaurant was open and been told there would be a table for them in another hour. Just the right amount of time to meander the steep cobbled street of the miniscule village — one two-story inn, one church, one bicycle shop/post office and six houses. The restaurant was in the inn and the bar was filled, the bicycle shop was closed, but the church was open.

The tall doors looked more than fit to keep out the robber hoards that Adie said once roamed, preying upon traveling tradesmen who dared to brave the roads without sufficient protection, which explained why the inn looked more like a small fortress than a hotel. Inside, the church was dark and chilly. Taylor was glad for her windbreaker.

"No electricity," Edward told her, pointing to oil lamps set in niches along the side walls. "None in the village."

"There's a generator for the refrigerator at the restaurant," David said. "The power comes up the highway but they didn't want the poles and lines to spoil the look of the village."

"The "highway", barely two lanes wide snaking around, barely clinging to the near vertical sides of the mountain, slipped by directly below the inn. Edward had pointed up at it just before they made the turn. A steep loop of road, maybe a quarter of a mile long had brought them into the village where they'd wedged the cars in, in what Taylor considered heroic examples of parallel parking, between three other black sedans and one very red Italian sports car. In front of the sports car there was a boxy modern tour bus. When they left the cars, Lars slung his knapsack casually over one shoulder.

Adie and her sisters dropped coins in a little wooden box and took votives to place in the holders on the rail where a dozen or so candles already flickered, casting dancing shadows on the crisp white on white embroidered altar cloth.

"For Petra," Marta whispered.

"For all our loved ones lost," Elsbeth added with a peek toward Edward.

"A custom," Adie said. "For God's blessings and long life."

"In that case," Chris said, delving in his pocket for coins, dropped a handful into the box and handed Taylor a candle, "...can't have too much of either of those.

For Petra. She thought, lighting the wick.

For Laszlo, also missing.

For the blessing that brought me Chris.

For a long life to enjoy him.

Not a very churchy kind of thought.
Sure it is.

Taylor lifted her eyes from the flickering flame to the altar and the stone crucifix above.

What thoughts, prayers, dreams, must have been brought here over the centuries.

After a bit they left the little church's stone walls leaping with shadows and crossed back over the cobbled street now slick with rain, to where a parade of happy people, laughing and joking in at least two different languages, were trooping out of the inn and onto the bus.

They were seated next to a window that overlooked the highway and below it a rushing stream and the gray granite side of a mountain where the last rays of daylight changed the golden shadows minute by minute. Dinner came, in course after course apparently preordered by David before they'd gone to the church. A hearty meat and vegetable soup for starters. Then a pork roast, chicken in a heavenly wine sauce, a layered pasta dish for which lasagna was too plain a term, creamy onion risotto, asparagus dripping in butter, zucchini dripping in Parmesan, honey glazed carrots, baby romaine lettuce in an herbed vinaigrette, hot bread, and four kinds of cheese. For dessert, fresh berries in custard. And, of course, there was wine, red, white and then red again and brandy followed by thick, strong coffee. All of it interspersed with lots of talk of old memories, praise for the food, and laughter. The blue knapsack hung on the back of Lars chair where neither Lars nor Chris paid it much attention but Taylor eyed it curiously more than once and speculated as to its contents.

For the first half of the meal her inner voices had preached caution, moderation, even abstinence but somewhere between an asparagus tip and a bite of succulent pork the voices lapsed into contented self-indulgence.

Go for it, practicality had proclaimed. *You can diet tomorrow.*

CHAPTER 15

It did occur to her, fastening her seat belt, that Edward had imbibed as heartily as any of them. The thought manifest into a real concern as they swayed into the curves, speeding headlong downhill on the wet pavement. If the road had seemed narrow for two-way traffic in daylight, it now felt a tight fit for a single car between the uphill wall of rock and low stone barrier that edged the drop off to the river below. Oncoming, a set of headlights beamed bright, Taylor braced.

Should have taken the candle lighting bit more seriously.

Edward did not slow, the oncoming lights did not flinch. She shut her eyes. Somehow, in a space for one, two passed. She remembered the tour bus, shuddered, then checked Elsbeth's face to see if she were also concerned. Elsbeth had fallen asleep.

Of course. The walk, the dinner, the wine.

Maybe she has ridden with Edward before.

Maybe she has already died of fright.

Another car whizzed by, squeezing through the impossible space beside them like some shape changing cartoon vehicle. In the front seat, Edward and Chris were discussing the virtues of the local wines. They rounded the inside of a hairpin turn and before Taylor saw it coming a tour bus, interior lights blazing, curious faces scoping them out, oozed by taking what, to Taylor, seemed an endless time to do so.

"Oooohhhh," she said, without meaning to.

"Don't worry, Taylor," Edward said. "The Swiss are very good drivers. You almost never see even a dented car."

That's because all the accidents are fatal - the cars total losses.

It was then she became aware of the car behind them. It hung on their bumper, the headlights filling the car with white light.

David? she wondered.

"Tourist!" Edward cursed. The "tourist" swung around them, leaning in so close Taylor was glad for recessed door handles. The car swayed toward the vertical wall of granite and they heard the scraping sound of metal on stone, it swung back toward them crowding them into the low stone barrier. She expected any second to feel the car smash through the wall and plunge down the bank and into the river. Side by side the cars negotiated a left curve and headlights were suddenly visible in the oncoming lane. The "tourist" swooped forward and slid in front of them with probable inches to spare as the oncoming car slipped by. Then, obviously still standing on the gas, the car disappeared into the rain. Taylor let out her breath — Edward never slowed — they were alone on the road again, only David's headlights far behind flashing into the rearview mirror in the long stretches between turns.

Did you see?

It was a black sedan!

You were too busy praying to be sure.

It was black.

It's dark, it could have been any color.

It was a tourist.

In a rush.

It was a black sedan.

Paranoid.

I may be paranoid but that doesn't mean someone isn't out to get me. The old punch line made her smile and she relaxed, not quite enough to doze off.

By the time they arrived back at the chateau, Taylor was more than ready for bed. Adie offered Campari but got no takers. The cars were unloaded, "thank yous" and "farewells" proffered all round and Edward and David departed with a smiling Elsbeth in the back seat. Even the climb to the second floor seemed a considerable trial and Taylor was glad for Chris's supporting arm.

"Tired?" he asked.

"Happily so," she replied.

"Well, hang in there just a minute longer. Lars and I need to check our mousetrap."

Taylor noted Lars had his knapsack tucked firmly under his arm. She sat on the edge of the bed undoing her shoes while Lars and Chris checked the room in general and the armoire in particular.

"Cheese is gone," Lars said gleefully.

"They could still be listening," Taylor reminded them, pointing to the ceiling.

"Our sneaky friend would be too anxious to get back to his companions and check out what we have to be sitting around in the dark once he's gotten his hands on our lists. Still..."

Chris pulled a large flashlight from the top of the armoire, "Shall we take a look round, they'll be expecting us to if they're anywhere where they can watch."

"I'll get my torch, too — so they cannot fail to see us looking," Lars said exiting.

"Darling, you get yourself to bed. This won't take long."

It took long enough for Taylor to fall asleep. She'd heard them faintly as they started up the steps, and again as they crossed from the new boards onto the old floor that was her ceiling. For a brief second the beam of one of the lights shone down at her as she climbed into the bed. Then her head hit the pillow and she was too sleepy to care what they found.

She was climbing higher, ever higher up a flight of stairs carved into the side of a mountain, hanging tight to the tail of the largest possible black and white cow. The top of the mountain was shrouded in clouds. Somewhere in front of the cow she could hear Chris talking with Lars but the cow was so wide she couldn't see around it and if she slowed to lean and try to see what lay ahead the cow bawled and jerked her onward. Eventually she and the cow were wrapped in the cloud — it felt thick and warm. She couldn't see her feet or anything of the cow but the tail in her hands and still they trudged upward. Taylor tried to call out to Chris but she couldn't make the words come. Then the cow was falling. Taylor was on her knees on the top of the stairs that had ended abruptly, watching the cow fall down, down, down, into the valley splashing at last into a miniscule pool at the bottom, apparently unharmed.

What do I do now?

Go down the stairs.

Jump, if the cow can make it so can you.

If all your friends jumped off a cliff would you do it, too?

When did I become my mother?

Go down the stairs.

It's too cloudy, I can't see the way.

And the cloud had become heavy, she couldn't get her feet to move through it.

Chris!

Chris where are you?

He jumped off the mountain.

He wouldn't — not without me.

Chris!! Taylor struggled, still unable to move beneath the weight of the thick, warm cloud.

"Shshhh. I'm right here."

"Clouds heavy," Taylor mumbled pushing at the blankets.

But the clouds had parted, she came just awake enough to know that, for the most part, she knew who she was and where she was and that Chris was there. She snuggled deeper into his side and let herself give up control to the dream as she floated softly down into the warm pool where Chris (and the cow) swam.

"I had the most amazing dream," Taylor said. It had been neither the bright beam of sun now dancing its way across the room nor the distant tolling of a tenor bell that woke her. Warm, possessive hands had tempted her from one happy place into another. If the dream had been pleasant the reality was sheer heaven. Close beside Chris, slightly sweaty, her breathing just beginning to return to normal, Taylor felt totally sure that this was how it always was between the two of them.

And if it isn't, I don't want to know.

She told him about following the cow up the steps.

"You always remember dreams. I never do," he said, a finger sketching idle circles around her left breast. "What do you suppose it means?"

"The dream or.."

"The dream," he told her.

"Probably that I am singularly impressed by the fact that cows can climb stairs."

"And leap from heights."

Chris leaned across to kiss her.

"Emmhuh," she mumbled thoroughly enjoying the kiss. "But I think it has to do with Laszlo being missing and the weird stuff on the third floor and black sedans like the one I think knocked me off the bike and the one last night and..."

"So, there were black sedans in your dream, too?" he asked between little kisses that had wandered off her lips and were sliding down her neck.

"No, not exactly but... Emmmm.... Aren't you supposed to be somewhere this morning?"

"Not today."

"Still, we can't exactly stay in bed. I mean..." Taylor was not at all sure she wanted to make the point.

"No, we can't, more's the pity. When we get this all wrapped up we are going straight home, and to bed, for a week."

"Sounds good to me," Taylor agreed, she ran a light hand down his chest, fluffing the scattering of tawny ringlets.

He kissed her lightly and threw back the covers.

"Come on. Lars has a bell tower for us to climb and a mechanical clock he says is not to be missed."

CHAPTER 16

With Marta and Adie already off to church, breakfast was a speedy affair; the coffee, a plate of warm sweet rolls, and the ever-present bread and cheese waiting on the table.

Taylor'd gone up to put away her pajamas and straighten the bed. On her way back she followed the sound of voices to find Chris and Lars examining the addition to the footprints on the flight to the third floor.

"We couldn't be sure last night, still can't. Did he go up and come down? Or come down and go up?" Lars said pointing at the prints that definitely overlapped all previous ones but not each other.

Lars and Chris's prints from the night before were overlapping at the far right edge.

"It doesn't make any sense either way," Chris said. "Why go up at all. We weren't home and our rooms are on the second floor."

"And if he came down first and then up," Taylor said nodding in agreed confusion, "How did he get up to the third story in the first place."

"Through Marta's," Lars said. "But that still makes no sense. Why the trip through the attics? Puzzles. Puzzles."

"How about the door on the landing?" Taylor asked.

"Not likely," Lars said going to take a large iron key from a ledge above the door.

The key turned with difficulty and the door creaked and screeched on rusty hinges as he pulled it open.

"A door to nowhere, well up, but not down. See, only steps to the top of the tower."

There was a narrow balcony and steps that curved up around the outside of the tower, neither with any railing to prevent a good fifty-foot drop to the ground below.

"Come," Lars said pushing the door shut and locking it. "If we hurry we can get up and down the bell tower and be right on time for the twelve o'clock show at the clock."

In under an hour they were parking the car in the cobbled square of a small walled town, larger than the mountain village of the night before, but not by much.

"Is good timing," Lars said, slinging the blue knapsack over his shoulder and striding off toward the plain, inelegant church that anchored one corner of the square. "See, eleven steps to the doors. Then ten more flights of eleven steps each to the top. It is famous."

"You up to this," Chris asked Taylor as they started after Lars.

"Had to have been more steps up the mountain yesterday. This should be a piece of cake."

They had to wait for one group to descend before they and about ten others were allowed to begin the upward climb. First stone steps, narrow, worn, twisting about an open core down which four stout ropes hung, the sturdy wooden balustrade blackened by time and the many hands that had smoothed its surface over the centuries. The last four flights were wooden, each steeper and narrower than the one before, the last being almost vertical, like a ship's ladder, leading up from the bell chamber to the stone rampart that surrounded the tower. From there they could see for miles over the town's walls.

"Handy, I imagine, a few centuries back," Taylor panted.

"They kept watch, in the beginning for bandits, then through the wars," Lars told her.

"Still handy," Chris said with a nod of his head toward the open square below where the car was parked.

Two men in dark suits stood next to their car, one with dark hair peered through the windows. The other, pale hair, almost white, worn in a neat ponytail fastened at the nape of his neck, tried the passenger side door and, finding it open, slid into the front seat for a look. He emerged empty-handed and the two walked off. Taylor leaned out, trying without success to get a look at their faces.

"Careful darling," Chris said, grasping her waist. "I do think we have them worried."

"Which means Laszlo has told them nothing they wanted to hear," Lars agreed.

The docent who'd led them up the stairs tinkled a small bell, the signal it was time to start down and they trouped after the others.

"Aren't you going to try to catch them?" Taylor hissed in her husband's ear that was conveniently nearer since he was a step ahead of her.

"Couldn't possibly get down before they disappeared, even if I slid down the rope," he hissed back.

They sauntered around the square reading the menu in the restaurant's window, sniffing in appreciation at the entrance to the coffeehouse, passing two candy stores only to be drawn into the third by the sight of a confectioner hand dipping chocolates. Chris bought a round box with an assortment of cream fillings in dark chocolate. Taylor bought a map of Switzerland at the bookstore and Lars bought pipe tobacco in a tiny little shop that smelled like the inside of a box of expensive cigars. There was still a half hour until noon so they had coffee at a café with outside tables shaded by green and maroon umbrellas directly across the wide square from the clock.

"We don't even know what they look like," Taylor lamented.

"We have pictures of several of Walter Altzen's friends but," Chris said, "there is a good chance he has others here we don't know about. That's not your worry. Relax and enjoy. This is not a sting, we're not after anyone for any particular crime. Just their money."

"They don't seem too pleased," Taylor said. "It must be a lot of money."

"Yes, indeed it is," Lars said, nodding. "Many hundreds of millions, its loss would severely restrict their plans."

"And, we hope, give time for them to be found and removed from polite society permanently," Chris said, "Our job is to identify the funds, provide proof they came from drug and other crime sources and secure its release to the appropriate agencies of the appropriate governments. Strictly paperwork and negotiations."

"And you were expecting them to let you do this without their interference?" Taylor asked.

"We had hoped they wouldn't know it was happening until it was too late. As it is, we have succeeded in having the majority of the funds frozen," Chris told her. "If they had our real lists, they would know which funds are not frozen, and which ones we haven't discovered."

"And they could move them," Lars shook his head, his Santa's beard ruffling. "If they have no money for guns, explosives, travel, the world gets a little safer. Every dollar we get perhaps we save a life. Now we must finish our negotiations and hopefully find out who is the leak, the spy that let our secret be known."

"And find Laszlo," Taylor added.

"And find Laszlo, or find out what happened to him," Chris stated flatly.

"Come," Lars said, standing, "We get a good place to watch the clock."

The clock tower wasn't all that tall. Twenty feet above the street a wide ledge connected a pair of shuttered doors to either side of the giant clock face. As Taylor and Chris followed Lars across the pavement toward the small but growing crowd at the clock's base, she caught a flash of movement out of the corner of her eye.

A black car!

Moving too fast for this crowed street.

Headed right for us!

"Chris!"

She yelled even as Chris grabbed her around the waist and pulled her back out of harm's way and Lars executed a nimble leap forward of the sort any Kris Kringle would be proud. Taylor felt the car swish by so close her tote knocked against the side just behind the long scrape that marred both of the driver side doors. Other pedestrians scrambled to get out of the way as the car sped on, passing under the portico and out of town.

"That was..." she gasped.

"Yes dear, I'm afraid it was," Chris said, taking her arm firmly, "Come on let's not miss the clock."

On the stroke of twelve the doors opened and a jolly Punch danced from the left, a rosy cheeked Judy from the right. Punch kissed Judy on one cheek and then the other. With each kiss Judy batted him with her rolling pin. Twelve kisses, twelve blows, each time to a different part of his body. Then they spun around each other and, Punch taking bows, Judy brandishing her rolling pin, they returned to their starting points. The whole time the show was going on cameras clicked, people laughed, and Taylor puzzled over the enigma of the prints on the stairs, and the probability that the black car that just tried to run them down was the same one that had tried to run them off the road the night before and, just maybe, the one that had knocked her off the bicycle.

CHAPTER 17

Lars drove them back to the chateau by a circuitous route, stopping for lunch at a hofbrau where they had short, fat sausages — the size of a man's fist — cooked with dark greens.

"Chard?" Taylor asked.

"Kale, very good for you," Lars said. "Very German."

Lunch also included pudgy soft rolls and a pale, pungent cheese that spread like cake icing and tasted heavenly once you got it past your nose.

Another thirty minutes in the car and Lars pulled into an empty parking lot next to a small hillock whose only feature, besides some volunteer bushes, was a flight of cement steps down into what at first appeared to be a cave.

"A tunnel?" Chris asked at the entrance, running his hand over the cut stone blocks that formed the walls and arched overhead. They could see daylight ahead.

"A Roman tunnel," Lars replied. "An arena. Small, but then the number of soldiers posted here was not great. Still the officers had to have their entertainment."

The trio emerged into the middle tier of a seven-tier circle, large stone blocks created wide benches like an upside down, inside out, wedding cake. Half the size of a football field, three sides looked much as they must have when the Romans took their leave. The fourth side was partially collapsed, more of the volunteer shrubbery poking out between dislodged blocks of stone.

"Gladiator fights?" Taylor asked, descending, with Chris's help to the arena floor.

"And plays, orations," Lars explained. "See the gladiators came in from there." He pointed to a rubble-filled arch on the collapsed side. "If you stand in the middle you can be heard, even at the top. Good acoustics."

There was a clear blue sky, tall trees waved in the slight breeze beyond the rim of the little coliseum and birds chittered.

Taylor sat on the cool stone and tried to imagine the sights that had played out on that dusty floor two thousand years before.

Men fighting each other — maybe to the death — as entertainment. Barbaric!

Football, boxing, action movies, reality TV - The world is still barbaric.

Blood and gore all over the floor and me without a spoon, the inner cynic chided.

The more things change the more they stay the same.

This is a theater, a cultural extension of their homeland.

Well you sure wouldn't want to sit around too long listening to Ovid from the lips of the early Roman Empire version of the USO.

"Hard," Taylor said, standing and brushing the dust from her derrière. "Cold goes right through you. Bet they brought cushions."

"What, or who, do you suppose they chained here," Chris said from where he and Lars had been examining a series of iron rings still set fast in the stone of the lowest tier.

"Slaves," Taylor ventured. "There's no barrier to protect the audience from lions."

"They used bears, and tigers too," Lars said.

"Any lion, tiger, or bear with good sense," Chris opined, "would be more likely to attack the guys lolling on the cushions than the fellows with the swords and spears."

With a sudden whoop and a plaintive, protesting whine of "Mama," a family of five poured into the arena, the three preteen boys roiling down the stone steps and spreading across the seating tiers like an invading army. Mama and papa followed sedately, smiling and nodding to those already in residence. Mama spread a blanket across a sunny section of stone and plopped down, her back against the tier above, to watch her children engage in not so mock battle in the center ring. Papa sat beside her and pulled out a paperback.

The amusements of ancient Romans had been replaced, or perhaps only continued. The middle boy had his older brother on his back in the dirt. The gladiator looked to the audience for a sign and, receiving a thumbs-down from Chris and Lars, gleefully plunged his imaginary sword home.

Another short ride through three small towns brought them to a moderately larger town with a forbidding looking castle at its center.

"An armory," Lars announced.

A defacto museum, the thrifty Swiss never throw anything out, so as the weapons of war evolved, the old were not abandoned, not scrapped, or turned into plowshares. From swords, battle-axes, and pikes to uzies and tanks they lined the walls of every corridor, filled every room, of the large fortified castle. The ten-foot thick walls, arrow slit windows, and heavy plank doors left Taylor looking for a curved stone staircase replete with Basil Rathbone, Errol Flynn, and clashing rapiers.

The courtyard was filled with bright annuals and ancient cannons. A quartet of olive drab World War II types flanking the central fountain. In a gilt ceiling salon they found glass cases full of the dress of war and warriors, leather and bronze shields, shiny armor suitable for round table wear, the rich costumes worn by the Swiss guard at the Vatican as well as more modern camouflage and detox equipment.

"I thought the Swiss were pacifists," Taylor said eyeing a wall-hung display of gas masks, past and present.

"Neutral, dear," Chris said. "There is a subtle difference. Every Swiss citizen, male and female is required to do national service, a year I think and then a week or maybe it's a weekend a couple of times a year. Remember David told us he's satisfying his requirement with the forest project. The Swiss are prepared to defend their homeland but historically refuse to take sides outside their own boundaries."

"Except for the Vatican," Taylor corrected.

"It is a mercenary situation," Lars said. "The Vatican pays, very nicely, but there are many Swiss who disapprove of even that."

"Piet," Taylor said suddenly. "I just remembered. Isn't that where Piet said he was going? His annual training?"

"Right you are," Chris nodded.

"You saw Piet," Lars said cocking a white eyebrow. "I have visited many times in the three years since he moved in but never have I seen the man. He travels a lot. Showing his works, installing them, Marta says."

"That's what he said, too," Taylor nodded. "Marta introduced us the morning we arrived. We were early and he was packing up his car. He promised to show me his work if he got back before we left. But I can't remember his face."

By the time they arrived back at the chateau wonderful smells were coming from the kitchen and Adie — who seemed to have given up completely on her boycott of life outside her own apartment — greeted them with a big smile and a tray of glasses, ice and Campari ready on the counter.

CHAPTER 18

Despite dreams — Punch and Judy in the forms of Edward and Adie running through the orchard cum forest and a chariot race in the Roman arena in which she rode a bicycle and the chariot of her competitor turned into a black sedan, scrape and all, which swooped past snagging her tote, then lapped around to haunt her back wheel — Taylor slept just fine. Even the morning light did not wake her. Not until Chris removed his arm from across her waist and slung his feet to the floor did she stir.

"Time to get up?" she mumbled, peering through barely parted eyelashes.

"Sleep in if you like. I'll tell Marta you'll eat later. Lars and I have to get going, need to see what progress the locals have made locating Laszlo and tie down some more of our nasty friend's funds."

"I'll be down in just a bit," Taylor said, stretching. "Chris," she said, as he was reaching for the door. "I've remembered almost everything, everything but what happened after we arrived here. I have a dreadful feeling something important happened that, if I could just figure it out, would help you find Laszlo and the people who hired the man in the river."

"I don't see how, darling. We were together constantly even after Laszlo and Lars arrived. You did spend one day with Marta, the first day of our negotiations, you said you spent it in the garden napping. Jet lag." He looked down into her upturned face and smiled, "However, you do have an endearing habit of catching the nuance of things, if it's important it will come to you."

By the time Taylor was showered and dressed Lars and Chris were half way through their breakfast of paper-thin pancakes rolled around fresh peaches and raspberries and sprinkled with powdered sugar served with well browned sausage patties and, of course, bread and cheese.

"Glorious calories," Taylor said, sitting down and eagerly digging in. "Going to need a long walk," she added around the first bite.

"It is Elsbeth's day at the doctor," Marta said. "She called to say Edward agreed to drop us off, then after we can go to the museum. A real museum, not a lot of old guns, but many centuries of local history, if you like? And we can go to the Restaurante' for lunch, it is a kind of soup kitchen."

"Soup kitchen?" Taylor asked, not too turned on by the idea.

"They serve only soup and bread, authentic, ancient recipes," Marta explained. "From Roman times."

"When soup was served to travelers, restoratives, or whatever the Latin version of the word is. I remember reading about it somewhere," Taylor said, her enthusiasm returning. "Sounds like fun."

"Sounds like a lot more fun than we will have," Lars said eyeing the almost empty platter of sausage.

He put his fork down with resolve and pushed away from the table.

"We must go. I am sure Herr Mellis will bring crullers again and my pants are getting tight. I will be scolded when I go home."

Chris and Lars left, the table was cleared, and Taylor went up to make her bed and get a jacket. By the time she returned, Edward and Elsbeth were turning in the drive.

Edward had instructed, insisted really, not once but three times, that they were to wait for Elsbeth and that she was to call him as soon as she got home. So it was that Taylor and Marta sat in the Spartan waiting room, all Twenty-first century chrome and Naugahyde, talking quietly while Elsbeth got what, Marta explained, was her quarterly check up with her counselor.

"To be sure she is not stressed, able to handle her life. To avoid another break down, Edward says."

"Edward seems very concerned about her," Taylor observed.

"It is half brotherly love, half self-interest," Marta said. "With Edward one is never sure whether one should hug him or kick him. More often I think kick."

They took a bus to the next town, a matter of two miles, and got off at the portico of a castle whose walls came right to the road.

Castle first, road second, an inner voice decided.

Road then castle, another voice argued. *Castles got built along trade routes to protect the travelers and collect tolls.*

They walked across a worn cobbled courtyard to the base of a tall stone tower. Square and built of precisely cut rectangular blocks, much larger than bricks but not so large as those of the armory, the tower and the surrounding three, four, and five-story wings it soared above once more cast Taylor into the world of her favorite late night movies.

Robin Hood.

A Connecticut Yankee in King Arthur's Court.

Bettie Davis as Elizabeth I.

"The tower was gutted by fire in 1952 and they thought at first it would have to come down," Elsbeth was saying. "That's when the museum was developed."

They dropped a donation in the box at the door and stepped into the cool interior. But it wasn't the chill that had Taylor staring openmouthed. The walls were white plaster, individual displays lit by spotlights installed on the red metal scaffolding that supported the open metal grillwork that constituted the floor above, and the floor above that, and many more floors as well. Metal stairs spiraled upward in the center.

"Thirteen floors, including the first. Each floor the artifacts of a century, sometimes two or three, starting here with the twentieth," Marta said. "The higher we go, the farther back in time."

"More interesting," Elsbeth added, "is that everything was found locally — within a few miles. Every time they took down an old house, or a piece of wall and dug foundations for new buildings they would dig first for knowledge of the past inhabitants."

For the first two or three floors the displays consisted mostly of bits of documents, furniture, tools, china, even jewelry that looked pretty familiar – somewhat mundane. As they rose the changes from century to century were subtle but fascinating – the pin on brooches went from hinged and locked to a crude safety pin type to a solid, fixed, and down right lethal looking straight pin. Tools also were increasingly elementary: wooden spoons and paddles, iron pot hooks and awls. And there began to be bones, people bones.

Taylor and Marta had their heads bent over a display of large bronze and silver stick pins set with both precious and semi-precious stones used to fasten noblemen's cloaks in the fourteenth century, or so the sign said, when Taylor caught sight of motion below. Peering down through the diamond web of the floors she noted, not for the first time other visitors making their way through the ages.

They really ought to have a sign at the door warning off women in skirts.

Quit looking down, you'll get dizzy.

Those two men look familiar.

All you can really see is the top of their heads.

One dark one pale just like we saw from the church tower.

Paranoid.

They tried to run over us.

Somebody tried to run over Chris and Lars. You were just in the wrong company.

Then why are they here?

I should do something, tell someone.

Who?

What?

Alarmist.

I'm sure of it.

But not so sure that she said anything to Marta and Elsbeth. They called her attention to a collection of polished metal hand mirrors with ornamented handles and, in the same case, several wooden and bone combs.

"Imagine getting those through your long tresses without a cream rinse," Taylor said.

They lingered over a display of daggers, some with blades a mere three or four inches long, some with jeweled hilts, all very dangerous looking, waiting for the group of school children on the floor above to move upward. Then the three continued the climb up the tower and down through the centuries. The men, whoever they were, stayed a steady two floors behind.

The tower had no real windows, now fitted with glass, the narrow slits were once meant to accommodate archers. Since the tower had been ten stories high and was fitted with a thirteen-story interior the slits were not always at a height that offered any kind of a view. When Taylor did get the opportunity to peer out, the only cars she could see were far below, half of them black sedans, and none of them, that she could see, with a scratch or scrape on the driver's side.

I know it's them.

The hair on the nape of her neck itched and it was with great effort that she kept from staring at the tops of the brown and blond heads below. Panic was curling its tendrils through her thoughts, her palms were moist, her heart begin to pump faster. They had passed no one headed down, Taylor tried to look up through the metal grills, past the mob of children with their chaperons.

You can't just go up thirteen stories and exit onto a cloud.

There was an exit door on the tenth floor and Taylor eyed it with longing as they trudged past and on up the stairs. Her panic continued to rise as they reached the twelfth floor and she saw the men still below them, cutting off their exit possibilities.

What are they going to do in broad daylight – with witnesses?

I don't want to find out.

Taylor's interest in local ancient history waned. Her attention divided between the children above and the two men below, she followed after the sisters who were too intent upon the displays to notice her distress. Elsbeth called Taylor's attention to a display of rough pottery shards and when she looked up the crowd of children had evaporated. The top floor, when they reached it, was deserted, housing only more bones, fossils, and crude tools, the artifacts covering far more than mere centuries of very ancient history. One diminutive mummified antecedent found still clutching a stone blade seemed almost as wary as Taylor felt.

"People were much shorter then," Elsbeth observed.

It was the door behind the short ancestor of bankers and chocolatiers, shepherds and cheese makers that caught Taylor's eye.

EXIT the sign said, and into a cloud or not, Taylor was anxious to do just that.

CHAPTER 19

One eye to the men below that were now taking the intervening steps two at a time not even pretending to be interested in the displays, Taylor followed Marta and Elsbeth out the door and then gulped. They were still on a metal grill platform, this one narrow, with the minimum of railing, hanging from the side of the ancient tower.

A fire escape!

Tell Marta.

You couldn't do this in a public building in Chicago!

Tell them both.

Tell them what?

Frighten them because you're afraid of blonde men?

Blonde men with ponytails.

Remember what happens when you get treated for an emotional breakdown in this country!

The troop of children and adults were now several stories below them, almost to the level where the metal stairs let out onto the top of the castle wall. The narrow stairs vibrated as enthusiastic young bodies clambered downward.

"A wonderful view," Marta said, pausing. "See, over there, the trees beside the river and there, the tower of the next castle up the valley."

"It's stores now, a shopping mall," Elsbeth explained.

"A great view," Taylor agreed clutching the thin pipe railing and casting a nervous glance behind. "I... the height, it makes me a bit nervous."

"Not far to go," Elsbeth said kindly, continuing to descend. "Don't look down, these steps are a little scary."

More than a little.

"And shaky," Taylor said, less concerned with looking down than looking up. It was still impossible to see their faces.

They could be anyone.

Tourists, even.

122

Taylor looked up again as she rounded the end of a flight and started down the next, she still couldn't tell if the blonde man had a ponytail. Her heart was racing.

You are getting all shook over nothing.

What's so unusual about a blonde guy in a suit?

Why would they be after you?

Why would anyone be after you?

They don't know I don't remember.

Remember what?

Maybe they want to get rid of you before you do remember.

Terrific.

The class trip spilled off the end of the fire-escape onto the broad top of the stone wall, still many floors above the ground and no railing at all on the inside edge, but four times or more as wide as the metal stairs.

And solid.

They'd come to a flight that jiggled more than the ones before. Elsbeth and Marta slowed. Taylor looked up - the men were closer, closing the gap.

"One to go," Marta said turning the last corner. "Who would think stairs would be such exercise. My legs are aching."

"Leftover aches from Saturday," Elsbeth said. "Don't tell Edward, but my legs cramped all day yesterday. We should find stairs to climb every day, to keep strong."

"Edward catches us running up and down the stairs and he will have us both locked away," Marta said, laughing.

Taylor had been too wrapped up in her suppositions about the two men to think of aches, even the one spreading across her chest. Nor did she let herself think of her increasing heartbeat.

No time to stop and take a pill.

Not until you get to the ground.

What? The two hoods are going to disappear when you're back on terra firma?

Aren't you going to be ashamed when the nice tourists tip their hats politely and wish you good morning!

They're not wearing hats.

Hats would make them look even more like Chicago hoods.

Chicago hoods on vacation in Switzerland.

Hoods with a job to do in Switzerland.

That possibility caused Taylor to make another attempt at seeing faces and the blonde's hairstyle. Hoods – drug dealers and terrorists, not necessarily from Chicago, would be exactly who would be worried about Chris's goals.

What did I see?

The men were at the top of the flight as Taylor turned - she didn't recognize either one of them. Neither did she stop to see if they would smile or greet her, politely or otherwise. She would feel safer on the stone walk, what could they do with all those witnesses, the children, right there? Unfortunately, she saw the last of the children's heads disappearing down steps a dozen yards on.

"You're right about the exercise," Taylor said, linking her arms through the two women's and picking up the pace. "It's made me hungry. I hope that soup kitchen isn't too far off."

There was a rattle of metal and a double thud as the men leapt down the last steps. Taylor looked over her shoulder to see the men rushing at them.

What?!!!

Taylor felt suddenly on the wrong end of a stampede.

They're going to knock you down!

They're going to push you over the edge!

Why? There had to be a reason.

What do they think I know?

They don't look to be in any mood to answer questions.

Do something!

"Look out," she yelled, pulling with all her might, hauling a startled Marta and Elsbeth with her, back against the outer wall of the parapet.

Closer to the sheer drop off of the inside edge than his companion, the objects he was set to throw his weight against suddenly removed from his path, the blonde looked surprised. Unable to stop the momentum he'd gathered, he flew past the women, hung a millisecond in space, then without even a scream dropped from sight to land with a sickening thunk on the cobbled courtyard several stories below just as the school group flooded from the bottom of the steps.

Elsbeth and Marta gasped and turned away.

The dark-haired man never paused, fleeing past the shocked women, past the stairs the children had taken, and on around the top of the wall, disappearing where the parapet turned around the side of another tower.

Lunch had to wait. The ambulance came and the police.

"A terrible accident," the museum people kept saying.

"Then why did the other man run off?" Elsbeth asked quietly, so that only Taylor and Marta heard her.

"To get to wherever they were rushing to on time," Marta said, in a cynical half whisper.

"Lunch reservations?" Taylor speculated wryly, unable to take her eyes from where the man lay crumpled his head twisted to one side. The rubber band had snapped and his long pale hair spread out hiding his face, the ends soaked in the pool of blood that spread beneath him. Taylor was almost as concerned by the dead man on the pavement as she was by the irrefutable fact that he had tried to kill her. She was not entirely certain she was going to feel at all like eating.

The police questioned the children and the adults with them first. It gave Taylor plenty of time to think about what happened and decide to leave it to Chris to tell the authorities what he pleased about their previous encounter with, she was certain, the same two men. When her turn came she answered the questions she was asked truthfully if not so fully as she might, especially when asked if she had seen the other man "push the blonde gentleman".

At lunch over a steaming bowl of lamb broth, thickened with barley and onions, served with thick slabs of firm, crunchy crusted bread and a glass of heady red wine it was impossible not to talk about the shocking occurrence. Again Taylor did not offer any of the suppositions flying around in her head.

A pair of huge soup pots hung on iron hooks in the largest fireplace Taylor had ever seen. The patrons were sitting on three-legged stools at tables whose tops were one big slab of wood bleached white with much scrubbing. It seemed entirely possible they had not climbed completely back into the Twenty-first Century despite the fact that the white bowls and ceramic handled soupspoons looked more Williams-Sonoma than ancient Roman or even middle Dark Ages.

"It is probable we will never know exactly what happened or why," Marta said at last. "It certainly made for an exciting morning."

"Oh my," Elsbeth sighed. "Edward may never let me go out again!"

CHAPTER 20

All through dinner Taylor watched the looks flash between Chris and Lars as she and Marta recanted their adventurous day.

"I have been to the museum several times since it opened," Adie said. "Old papers, old bones, and broken bits of pottery for the most part. Never anything so exciting as a dead man."

"It is Taylor's second body since she's come," Marta said, pouring a glass of wine.

"Not mine!" Taylor said. "Not either one of them."

"Of course not, dear," Chris said, but Taylor heard an underlying tone in his voice that concerned her.

"I believe I have some calls to make," Lars said, pushing away from the table.

"Without your dessert?" Adie asked surprised. "Are you not feeling well?"

"You save me a slice, make that two, of the pie. Strawberry rhubarb is a favorite of mine. You know that. And save me some ice cream to go on top, too, please. I will have it when I have finished with my telephoning."

He looked at his watch.

"I want to get at it before everyone has settled in for the evening."

Chris walked Lars to the door where they conversed quietly and then rejoined the women at the table to enjoy a large slice of the sweet-tart dessert warm from the oven with a large scoop of vanilla ice cream perched precariously on the latticed top. He ate it slowly, savoring every bite.

Taylor wanted him to hurry up — she had a zillion questions begging to be asked. Questions she knew she shouldn't broach in Marta and Adie's hearing. She bolted her pie and ice cream and sat sipping impatiently at the remainder of the wine in her glass. The three women cleared the table while Chris started on a second slice of pie and ice cream.

Taylor looked daggers at him while removing the breadboard and the remainder of the cheese. Chris squeezed her elbow and smiled up at her sweetly, a twinkle in his eyes that brought back a flood of memories. Something was going on, something he would tell her about in his own good time. He was worried. That was in his voice. But it was coming together — she hoped — that was what the twinkle was about, if she was remembering correctly.

Chris was still savoring his seconds when Lars returned.

"I have earned my dessert," the big man said, settling into his chair.

He handed Chris a piece of paper scrawled with cryptic notes. Despite her closeness beside her husband on the bench Taylor could not get a clear enough look at the page to make any sense of it.

"Ah," Lars hummed, accepting the remaining third of the pie, still in its ceramic pan piled with two great scoops of ice cream melting ever so slightly around the edges.

"I kept the pie warm in the oven," Marta told him. "Now, it is time for our favorite game show, Adie and I do not miss it, not even to clean the kitchen. We do the dishes later, maybe in the morning."

The last was said with a nod toward Taylor, a reminder that the kitchen was still Adie and Marta's private space.

"You have a good night's sleep," she said, still talking to Taylor, "These men can solve their problems without worrying you."

"Good night," Taylor called after Marta's departing figure.
But I'll worry anyway.
You won't let them keep you out of it.
They'd best know better than to try.
Or you'll what?
I'll...

"Taylor?" Chris called her back from her interior musings. "I presume you have figured out the two at the museum were the same men that poked around our car and tried to run us down yesterday. Colleagues of the late, waterlogged, Walter Altzen."

"But why?" she asked. "I mean, yesterday I thought they were after you two. When I first spotted them today I presumed they were just following me, that they'd missed you somehow and knew if they stuck to me they would be led back to you or..."

"We thought we'd lost them," Lars said between bites.

"And we hadn't wanted to," Chris said. "We'd planned on having a talk with them. But it's obvious now that they were at least as interested in you as they were in us."

"Why?" Taylor demanded.

"I have no idea." Chris stood and took his empty plate to the counter. "We've been together nearly every minute since we arrived, or you've been with Marta. Were they trying to push her off the wall, too?"

Taylor thought for a minute.

They were running at us, the two of them like a couple of linebackers.

But who did they think had the ball?

They could have easily knocked us both off the wall, and Elsbeth as well. Were they intent on just one of us?

On me?

"At the risk of repeating myself, why?" Taylor asked.

"If we assume it has something to do with Laszlo's disappearance," Lars said, "then perhaps there is something you, you and Marta, have seen that meant nothing to you but would to us."

"But we went over that before. I've told you everything - everything I remember anyhow."

"It could be they only think you saw something," Chris said. "Either way I think I'm going to stick around tomorrow and keep an eye on you myself. We'll go shopping in Italy. Lars can deal with Herr Mellis and the crullers."

"But your negotiations..." Taylor said, thinking how important it was to stop any dollar that might be used for terrorist purposes.

"Are all but concluded. Just lots of fine print to get through," Chris told her.

"And I am very good with the fine print," Lars said, scraping his fork around the nearly empty pie plate to pick up the last morsels of flaky crust and fruit.

"However, that is for us to know and no one else to find out," Chris said sternly. "If our playmates knew, they might think they had no further use for Laszlo and then..."

"Who am I going to tell?" Taylor asked. "Do you really think Laszlo is still alive?"

The thought of Laszlo being dead brought her sudden grief.

You don't even remember what the man looks like.
But he must have been important to me.
So important you don't remember how you met.
Don't even remember seeing him since you arrived here.
He saved my life.
You made that up.
I remember that.
When?
How?
I don't remember that part. But he did.
Does Chris know about this?

Taylor remembered being held close by the tall dark Russian. She had been in danger, great danger, and he had saved her. She couldn't remember his face or what the danger had been, not even if it had been a few days ago or perhaps months, years before. But she remembered feeling safe with him.

"Laszlo would take a lot of killing," Lars said confidently. "And they would want to keep him alive, as long as they think there is anything to be gained by stopping us."

"So," Taylor said. "You are going to go eat crullers with Herr Mellis and we are going to Italy. To shop. And to see if Walter Altzen has any more friends that want a try at killing us - me."

"Exactly. Clever girl," Chris said, taking her hand and helping her rise from the bench.

"But..." Taylor said, feeling there was something yet unsaid, unasked perhaps, but she was unable to put it in words. "What about Marta and Adie. What if they — Walter Altzen's friends — come here?"

It wasn't precisely what was niggling at her but it was a concern.

"I will make some more phone calls before I go to bed. They will be safe. I promise," Lars said. "If the dark-haired man, or anyone else comes near the chateau, they will be arrested and held for a chat."

"Bedtime, darling," Chris said, steering her toward the door. "Tomorrow my credit cards and I will be at your full disposal. You know how much I love to shop."

Taylor remembered with no problem at all that when Chris came with her they bought twice as much — spent three times as much — as she would have alone.

You get thoroughly exhausted just trying things on.

He spoils me.

So, you think you remember him well enough to trust him completely.

Certainly, I love him.

Not the same thing.

He loves me.

The thought pleased her no end and she leaned across to kiss his cheek.

"What was that for?" Chris asked her.

"I just remembered how nice it is that you love me."

"My pleasure I assure you," he said, grinning. "Does that mean I can get you to take a walk in the moonlight with me before we go up to bed?"

"What about Lars? Don't you have to help him or..."

"I am going to make a few more telephone calls and then check over the small print so that I can keep the bankers busy and the kidnappers convinced that negotiations are ongoing. Then I am going to get my beauty sleep," Lars said, eyeing the empty plate wistfully. "That was a wonderful pie," he sighed and hefted himself to his feet.

A nearly full moon paved the gravel road in silver pebbles and cast deep shadows between the mounds of zucchini and darker ones still between the long rows of grapes. They held hands, not needing to talk as they walked toward the place where Taylor had found herself in the ditch. There were gentle night sounds, wind through the trees, crickets, a dog far off. And smells, the musty sweet breath of the vineyard, the somehow green aroma of the zucchini, damp dirt mixed with roses and lavender, peppery chicory mixed with rosemary, sage and basil.

Taylor paused opposite the dark shuttered house in the vineyard and studied the ditch and the width of the road. She raised her head to see pinpricks of light through the trees about as far ahead as they had come.

"Another chateau," Chris said. "Marta said it was built at the same time — give or take fifty years — as theirs. I guess the Italians were not exactly welcome in the neighborhood — invaders. They liked to be within sight of each other — for safety."

"Marta told us that right before I rode off on the bicycle, didn't she?" Taylor asked, sure she was right. "And the bicycle belonged to Elsbeth's son. Marta keeps it hidden in the garden shed so Edward doesn't take it away. Now if I could only remember what happened here."

"You think it has something to do with Laszlo's being missing and the dead men," Chris stated rather than asked.

"Makes as much sense as any other possibility I can come up with. Do you suppose they ran me off the road because I saw something or did I see something when they accidentally ran me off the road?"

"That's pretty chicken and the egg. It could be something you and Marta saw, or might have seen, when you found the first body. Let's see who gets followed and/or watched tomorrow. If they all come traipsing after us and leave Marta and the chateau unwatched we'll have narrowed the possibilities."

"You mean tomorrow I'm bait?"

"Taylor, darling, you'll be absolutely safe. I promise, I'll be with you, and we won't be alone." Chris squeezed her hand reassuringly.

"But Adie and Marta will be bait too," Taylor said alarmed.

"They won't be alone either. I'm still more than curious as to how our visitors manage to get up to the third floor without leaving a trail of some kind."

"When we know how they got in," Taylor said, "I bet we'll know how they got Laszlo out."

"Agreed."

There was a rustle in the vineyard and Taylor heard a quiet cough.

"Chris!?" Taylor said, stiffening, heart beginning to race.

"It's all right. That's a friendly cough, you should have guessed they'd be watching. Let's go back now. No sense allowing the bad guys to get close enough to hear what we're saying."

Friendly cough!?

Bad guys getting close!?

"Chris," Taylor said her voice only a little edgy.

133

"I wanted to see if they were still interested, the bad guys that is," he said lightly.

They were walking back toward the chateau. The dog that had fallen silent began to bark again joined by another dog even farther away.

"And to keep our side on its toes. Looks like we can turn in without a worry in the world."

"Hummmm," Taylor replied, ears straining to hear anything but crickets, dogs, and wind, once she caught the gurgle of the river but no sound she could identify as human.

Ask him if he expects us to be attacked in Italy.

Of course he doesn't.

Of course he does - that's what bait is for.

Just how many friends did Walter Altzen have?

Maybe tomorrow we divide and conquer.

Maybe tomorrow I'll find some nice Italian shoes.

A leather jacket for Chris.

Pasta bowls.

"How difficult would it be to ship pottery home?" Taylor asked, trying not to sound like she was talking to impress a wider audience.

"For you, anything," Chris said. "The magic word being ship. I refuse to try and carry on anything larger than my briefcase."

Walking back up the driveway, dark because the trees shaded it from moon-glow as efficiently as, during the day, they blocked the sunlight, another quiet cough greeted them from the blackness beside the garden shed. Chris neither paused, nor turned his head, a firm hand on Taylor's elbow, he steered her forward to the welcoming glow of the porch lights.

CHAPTER 21

An army of armor clad men with flowing blonde hair dripping blood chased her up a never-ending staircase of expanded metal, the diamond shaped holes getting larger and larger until Taylor was sure her foot could easily slip through. Iron swords with jeweled hilts and arrows shot from cross bows sped past her head. Marta and Elsbeth, totally unaware of the danger led her higher and higher. At last a wizened warrior, in tattered rags lifted his hide shield, stemming the onslaught and Taylor fled past him onto a narrow platform whose only exit was more, steeper, jiggly, flights of expanded metal steps. This time barely wide enough to pass, the metal mesh frail, bending under her weight, the rail tearing away at her touch.

You're dreaming, wake up!

Not a dream — a nightmare.

But she did not wake up. Marta and Elsbeth marched stolidly onward, Edward now at their heels with a giant striped umbrella on a long pole he attempted to keep over their heads. The blonde army had overcome her defender and clattered down after her causing the dissolving structure to shake even more.

This is ridiculous.

Open your eyes!

Taylor was on a bicycle sailing through the dimly lit soup kitchen where both pots bubbled with polenta, the hot corn meal mush popping great lava like bubbles and spitting steaming motes. A young girl plucked at her clothing as she passed and then turned away to stir diligently at first one pot and then the other with a wooden paddle.

A kitchen tool from the thirteenth century.

What does the girl want from you?

Where did they go?

Who? Who are you looking for?

Laszlo.
Walter Altzen's friends.
The man in the black sedan.
Petra.
Chris.

"Chris," Taylor forced the word through her sleepy mind wishing, wanting, willing them to be a real out loud plea for release from the dream that held her captive.

"Uhuhum."

Taylor heard the response, felt the arm across her middle curl, pulling her closer into the warmth of her husband's side. Not quite awake it was still enough. Nightmare subsided into dream, the soup kitchen morphed into a ballroom where she whirled in Chris's arms to unheard music.

They were still dancing when the morning sunbeam came to wake her.

Lars dropped them off at the dock where a blue and white ferry, not new but well cared for, bobbed gently on the lake waters, and they got in line, boarding with dozens of others. It was relatively easy to tell the tourists from the locals – tourists tended to come in couples, clothing fashionable if not obviously new. Locals varied from women in worn coats with empty string or canvas shopping bags tucked under their arms greeting each other with laughter and the latest gossip, to suit clad men, briefcase in one hand and a newspaper in the other. She tried to spot the watchers, knowing they must be there, bad guys and good guys, just as Chris had said there would be.

Some of the guys could be gals.
Terrorists do not often come from a liberated society.
OK, no bad gals.

Sitting at the dock, the diesel engines churning up an impatient froth and putting out a foul smell, Taylor was regretting the trying of Lars' favorite cured, but not cooked, bacon at breakfast.

Do you look as green as you feel?

Then the gate was shut, the gangplank withdrawn, and the vintage wooden craft pulled away toward the middle of the long lake. The forward motion and a pleasant breeze paired to leave the diesel smell a mere smudge wafting to the rear. A running travelogue in Italian, French, English, German, and a fifth language Taylor was unable to figure out – she knew it wasn't Spanish – named the various small islands and pointed out a wide assortment of castles, chateaux and gardens in everything from pristine fresh painted and planted glory to abject ruin.

It was a long, slow, delicious trip under sunny skies. Taylor let the good guys and the bad guys worry about each other and relaxed on the wooden bench, Chris's arm draped around her shoulder, as they sipped hot tea bought from the vendor. The day was beautiful and she was going shopping in Italy – Taylor loved every minute of the two plus hours it took.

"Some of the Italians can be bad," Marta'd cautioned. "Check to see the label doesn't say Taiwan or Made in Japan."

"And hold your purse close," Adie added. "There are thieves. There are also lots of good bargains. The Italians are fine craftsmen, but they have no respect for you if you are not careful and bargain. They will act insulted, it is a game."

When they stepped ashore Taylor snugged her tote up under her arm and followed the crowd eagerly. The housewives and businessmen dispersed immediately to their errands and offices, the tourists milled, melting slowly into the narrow streets and alleys past the street vendors and the heavy aroma of Italian coffee and yeasty pastries.

Up the first narrow alley Taylor found a garlic press in a basket of kitchen gadgets sitting on the sidewalk outside a shop door and bought two, one to give and one to keep. Around the next corner they found an entire street full of pottery shops. Chris followed smiling while she wandered in and out of doors, deciding at last on a dozen blue and turquoise decorated, wide, flatish bowls good for soup, pasta, or salad and a giant oval platter bordered in the same pattern around a scene of the lake. Chris haggled expertly in Italian — a language Taylor was sure she had never known he spoke — and then contrived for the proprietor to crate the goods and have it delivered to the ferry extracting a written receipt to guarantee it would occur. When the bargaining was over, the shopkeeper clasped Chris's hand and thanked them for their patronage with a happy grin.

"Almost like home," Taylor said, thinking of the open markets in Mexico.

They had a delicious lunch — pork and mushrooms baked in a crust served with a warm salad of green beans and odd little pasta in garlicky herb vinaigrette — then they shopped some more. Taylor bought several fine wool scarves large enough to be evening wraps. Gifts. One scarf, deep red with swirls of purple and lavender Taylor knew when she saw it was perfect for her mother.

You're always wrong.
It's too tasteful.
The statue of the little boy peeing was too heavy to carry.
And she probably already has one.

In a small square, curtained booths offered a wide variety of leather goods. After much deliberation Taylor tried her own hand at haggling and then watched the dour vendor's face turn all smiles and nods as Chris paid him. She stuffed her tote into the new and slightly larger leather patchwork version of her faithful bag and they continued to browse.

Chris was in the process of trying on a caramel suede jacket, "perfect color, perfect fit" the vendor repeated in reasonable English. Taylor was watching, at ease, forgetting about the new tote fat with her purchases that swung from her shoulder.

"This one I think," Chris began to slip the jacket from his shoulders, "if the price is right."

Taylor felt a hand close on her arm, felt a warm, musky, unpleasant breath on her neck.

"Chris...!" But before she could complete the cry for help a motor scooter swooped through the crowded aisle directly at her and Taylor saw the sun glint off the blade of a knife. She drew in a frightened gasp.

He wants my new purse!

Is he with bad breath?

Bad breath wants you, you dummy.

Me?!

Duh! He wants to kill you.

Which one?

Either or both.

Angry, defensive, afraid, she stepped backward, away from the onrushing blade, feeling at once toes, not her own, beneath her feet as she and whoever was behind her fell sideways. In the scramble to right Taylor, both men disappeared. Momentarily two knives lay on the pavement to be removed by quick hands as a crowd gathered.

"Well," Taylor got out indignantly as Chris pulled her to her feet, not so much brushing her off as feeling for damage. "That was exciting."

The leather vendor was abashed to the point of accepting Chris's first offer on the jacket. Chris on the other hand, once he had ascertained Taylor was whole, seemed totally relaxed. Taylor's inner voices clamored for information but she hushed them knowing Chris would explain in good time. Three booths down they bought a pair of large square slipcovers for floor cushions and headed back toward the ferry dock.

There was already a line queuing up for the ferry they'd arrived on but first Chris wanted to be sure the pottery had been delivered. He fell into deep discussion with the ferry's purser with much motioning to the two medium sized wooden crates that sat in plain sight next to the gangplank. Chris inspected them carefully, going so far as to take out his pocketknife and wedge open one of the lids. Behind them the line lengthened and then began to file aboard the boat. Taylor took note of one man who hung back, repeatedly letting others precede him. The ferry captain announced last call in all five languages just as Chris and the purser seemed to come to some agreement and the crates were hefted aboard.

"Time to go," Chris said, taking her hand. There was a last minute rush of passengers, two men at the end of the line sweeping the man who had been being so polite in front of them onto the craft. As the three men passed, Taylor smelt an unpleasant whiff of musky breath, she hesitated.

"No, dear," Chris said, steering her away from the gangplank.

The purser climbed aboard, dropped the gate in place, and almost at once the boat began to move.

"I thought you would enjoy taking the airfoil back."

On the ferry the "polite" man had not yet given up trying to get back past the two men who didn't appear to understand what he was saying no matter how many different languages he used to order them out of his way.

"Airfoil?" Taylor asked, still watching the scene on the stern of the ferry as it chugged out into the lake.

"We'll get back in half an hour, forty-five minutes tops, plenty of time to organize someone to watch over our new friend. Then we can have a nice drink at one of those lakeside cafes and wait for our pasta bowls."

He shifted the hand carrying the bags with their leather purchases and led her along the dockside to another line of people boarding a much larger and extremely modern boat.

In short order the airfoil, with twice the ferry's load of passengers nosed out into the lake, picked up speed, rose up out of the water, and shot forward passing far starboard of the slower ferry. The islands, castles, chateaux, and gardens slid behind them at a fantastic pace. Taylor sat back in the soft seat feeling she'd had a very James Bond sort of day.

Chris returned to the tiled table under the green canopy that sheltered a dozen or so tiny tables filled with people, most sipping Campari, the strong artichoke based liquor that comes in many flavors.   A plate of savory canapé's barely left room for the glasses.

"Chores all done," he announced, sitting.   "Lars will pick us up later so we have nothing to do but enjoy the view and wait for the ferry to arrive."

Taylor looked through the wrought iron fence that separated the tables from a narrow strip of sidewalk, the road, and ultimately the docks.   Marine facilities of every description lined the waterside though farther along she could see a rocky beach.   A road hugged the lake edge and a seeming endless line of cafés, hotels and restaurants hugged the road.

"What if he sees us?   The man with the stinky breath. Will he try again?"

"I expect, when he arrives, he'll be too anxious to make his excuses to those that hired him to do much looking around.   The fingerprints on his knife identify him as a Syrian national named Bellas by the way, and a very prestigious hit man, not one of the bumbling moneymen who keep ending up dead.   Like to be a fly on the wall when he tries to explain why you're still alive.   But," Chris's face darkened, "he will, given the chance, try again."

"And we are going to give him that chance?" Taylor asked, none too pleased with the idea.

You were shopping — Chris was fishing.
You knew that.
I was having fun, I forgot. Sue me.
He's still fishing.
You're still bait.
Anything to be helpful.

"Not much of one," Chris reassured her. "However, before we pick him up we want him to take us to his bosses, maybe to where they have Laszlo. You're in no real danger darling."

"What about his friend on the motorbike, he had a knife, too?"

"He was only after your purse," Chris said, signaling the waiter for a refill for Taylor. "Bad timing on his part. You were distracted watching me try on the jacket and I was more or less helpless with my arms half down the sleeves. You were an easy mark, or so he thought."

"So, I was about to be stabbed from two directions!"

"The purse thief would have slashed the strap on the purse and maybe your arm in passing. Bellas' more likely would have got you in the back or through the ribs to your heart. He likes knives. Very quiet, efficient in a crowd. Generally he can be long gone before anyone notices the victim."

"Then this victim is grateful for the purse snatcher," Taylor said, trying not to think about the choice Bellas might have made.

"Don't be. Be grateful to the nice Italian man from Interpol who pulled you out of the way of the purse-snatcher and knocked the knife out of Bellas' hand. He's the one, with his partner, who picked up the knives, got them off to their lab and then kindly made sure Bellas didn't miss the ferry. Remind me to add them to our Christmas list when we get home."

CHAPTER 22

"I, also, have had a good day," Lars said, when Chris, with only a minor amount of interruption from Taylor, had finished explaining the results of their shopping trip. "As you know our banker friends have been more inclined to give us names for numbers than numbers for names. Without numbers we cannot get at the money and without names it is difficult for us to prove our case — that the money came from illegal sources. This morning we got word that a serious search of the current abodes of two of the names we received last week have yielded several additional numbers, which apparently are tied to many of the names already on our list and lots and lots of money. There are about to be another eight surprised and unhappy middlemen who, as Lazslo has suggested, may be more pleased to make a deal with us than have to try to explain the missing resources to their terrorist friends."

"But nothing new about Laszlo?" Chris asked.

"Alas, no, I am afraid his trade value is dropping. They are bound to know soon that we have cleared out the accounts we initially identified and are digging our way deeper into their funding system."

Lars heaved a mighty sigh.

"It is what Laszlo said could be done. Now I fear it has, or will soon, cost him his life."

"Maybe Bellas..." Taylor began hopefully and then lapsed into silence.

If Bellas is as good as Chris said, he'll know he's being followed.

Why would he go back and tell them he failed?

If he's smart he'll just leave the country and not report back at all.

Why not just try again, he knows where we live.

Cheery thought.

If at first you don't succeed, try, try again.
I wish he liked guns – I hate knives.

"I'd still like to know why and how," Taylor said.

"Why they want to kill you and how they got Laszlo out of the chateau, me too," Chris said. "But Bellas is unlikely to know in any case. I'd bet he was hired to do just one job, kill you. He didn't even arrive in the country until yesterday. Our best hope right now is that he will lead us to someone who does know."

"And then?" Taylor asked.

"Then we'll ask them a whole lot of questions," Lars answered.

"And in the meantime," Chris said, "I think we should be prepared for another visit. Nothing I was told about Bellas indicates he will let a little setback like this afternoon put him off his hunt."

"Stout fellow," Taylor grumbled, "It's always good to have a strong sense of purpose. You don't mind if it has me a bit unsettled."

"Let me remind you darling that I have a rather strong sense of purpose myself."

Chris turned in his seat to smile at her.

"However you managed to get yourself in the middle of this mess," he held up a hand to stop the protest he could see coming, "I have no intention of losing a very satisfactory wife."

"Satisfactory!" Taylor yelped.

"Very satisfactory," Chris repeated. "Perfect if only you weren't so prone to getting snarled up in things of a decidedly dangerous nature."

"It's a talent," Taylor quipped.

Lars roared with laughter and Chris and Taylor joined him as they cruised slowly through the narrow streets on the way back to the chateau.

A block before the railroad station they passed a black sedan going in the opposite direction. Taylor felt an instant leap of interest, the sun glinted off the windows and it was impossible to see more than the outline of the men in the other car, but she could see that the near side passenger had quickly turned his head away.

Means nothing.

Could be anyone, there's a zillion black cars in this tiny country.

Paranoid.

Look who's talking.

That car didn't have a scrape.

"Taylor?" Chris asked. "You OK?"

"I keep looking at black cars," Taylor said. "That one didn't have a scrape."

"They're checking the repair shops. Haven't found it yet," Chris said. "I don't think it will be seen out on the streets, they'd know we're watching for it."

Adie and Marta had enjoyed a totally unremarkable day as per their report and the confirmation of the invisible guardian angels whom Taylor suspected Chris had conversed with while she was washing up for dinner.

"Absolutely no one came anywhere near the chateau all day. There was a suspicious fellow hanging out for a while down under the bridge where you found the first body," Chris said slipping an arm around her as they stood under the stone porch arches, watching the twilight creep across the garden. "Turned out to be the cowherd waiting for his girlfriend."

"I did not find the body, not by myself. We, Marta, Marc — the cowherd — and I were all there. I never got near it. Didn't see the face, not clearly. Couldn't tell you a thing about it except it was probably male, and undoubtedly dead," Taylor concluded.

"Don't bite," Chris said, laughing. "I meant 'you' in the plural."

"I was just trying to eliminate the finding of the body as the cause of any great desire to see me dead," Taylor said. "I mean, if it were something about finding the body they would be after Marta and the boy too, right?"

"One would think so," Chris agreed. "Maybe in the morning you and I should take another walk up the road and see if we can spark some memories."

The shadows in the garden had joined those from the trees over the drive to lap at the steps. Two golden rectangles of light spread across to the porch's edge, marking the boundary between the dangers in the night and the safe haven of the ancient chateau.

"Do you suppose dinner is ready," Lars said, joining them from the stairs. "Lunch seems a very long time ago and I have been too occupied to have so much as a cup of cocoa since."

"Run out of pastries did we?" Taylor teased.

"Very early on today. There was an army of accountants, lawyers, and nervous three piece suited managers of departments with long and unenlightening titles attracted by our new list of numbers."

"But they agreed?" Chris asked. "You said you had a good day. The funds are frozen?"

"Until we can complete the proof of source. What must be negotiated yet is the legitimate ownership. Naturally the banks are concerned that such great sums should not be removed precipitously. Dinner is ready. I smell chicken."

The large man half turned toward the door lifting his white bearded face to sniff the air.

"You are truly hungry," Taylor said, "to smell chicken through stone walls.

Lars had been correct. It was ready and it was chicken. Chicken in a lemony wine and mushroom sauce served with oven roasted potatoes and onions, red chard sautéed with garlic and a huge green salad, and bread and cheese, of course. Marta was filling the glasses with the Merlot that accompanied every evening meal as they entered. Lars could barely contain himself long enough for the blessing to be sounded, the sweet silver peal of the bell still hung in the air as he stabbed his fork into a succulent piece of thigh. Without hesitation he added a leg before reaching for the bowl with the browned potatoes and caramelized onions.

After dinner it was Lars and Chris that walked in the garden. Taylor helped clear the table and sat on a stool at the end of the long counter, as near to being "in" the kitchen as she had yet been invited.

"Do you know, is Piet due back soon? I would love to have a good look at his work."

"He didn't say," Marta said. "But then he never does. We do not see him for weeks sometimes."

"I was unsure in the beginning," Adie said. "To have someone else in the house after father worked so long to get all the others out. But Piet convinced me, and he has done a fine job of remodeling that part of the chateau and is here so seldom and so quiet when he is."

"And just a renter, remember," Marta put in. "Should we want him gone he will go. Until then there is a nice income to pay our taxes and help with repairs. You did the right thing."

"I am agreed, Marta. You need not sell the idea so hard." Adie finished drying the large platter so recently piled with chicken and placed it behind the raised rail at the back of the counter next to the stove, which kept it and two other platters from slipping. They were not a set but there was crimson and gold evident in the pattern of each. "There was once a soup tureen," Adie said, "That matched the big platter."

"And bowls. I think there still are one or two," Marta added. "But Petra broke the tureen."

"Mother was angry with me because I let Petra help me and she dropped it." Adie smiled. "Petra never wanted to do her own chores. Like any child, she always wanted to do the things she wasn't old enough, big enough, to do yet. And she begged to help me, promised she'd be careful. She got it dried, and the lid. It was when she tried to put it on the shelf, she wasn't tall enough, and the lid slipped off and smashed and it surprised her so she dropped the tureen as well. She cried so hard. She cried the whole time mother was scolding me."

Adie stopped drying the plate in her hand and Taylor knew she was more than half a century away remembering the sister so long gone but not forgotten.

"Tomorrow is Tuesday," Marta said. "Adie will have the dairyman's daughter — another cheese lesson — and I go to Elsbeth's for lamb shanks. Lars tells me he takes you to the alehouse for rancet — fried cheese. Elsbeth will be sorry not to see you."

Taylor thought to protest that she would prefer the lamb shanks.

And put Marta and Elsbeth in harm's way?

The conversation continued around food in general and cheese in particular until the kitchen was spotless and, as if on cue, Chris and Lars returned.

"I think, please, I could find space for that last apple now," Lars said, "With maybe a bit of ice-cream if there is any."

In short order Marta had dished up the last of the evening's dessert, a plump baked apple stuffed with raisins and nuts, brandy sauce, thickened from its sojourn in the refrigerator, oozing down the sides to pool in the bottom of the dish. The scoop of vanilla ice cream slid off the top of the apple and nestled into the sweet, golden goo.

CHAPTER 23

Knives filled the air like angry wasps and Taylor ducked right and left unable to find a place to hide. The flapping canvas curtains of the leather stalls offered no protection at all. Piles of purses, shoes, jackets, and belts melted and the terror of her situation had her heart racing. At last Chris pulled her behind a pile of pillows and her heart slowed. Soon she was sitting on the floor eating stuffed apples from gold and crimson trimmed bowls with a bright-eyed girl whose dark hair hung in sleek plaits tied at the end with lavender ribbons. Then the two of them played hide and seek among the covered works in Piet's studio. Taylor dutifully counted, keeping the numbers in order with some difficulty, before she went looking. As she pulled each dropcloth away, Taylor found neither little girl nor piece of sculpture. Beneath the cloths were piles of money, piles that grew as they were uncovered and quickly reached heights where they became unstable and swayed threateningly over her head. The money began falling, the swarm of knives returned and still she couldn't find the little girl with plaits and lavender ribbons.

Bad dream!

No kidding.

Wake up! Chris, help me. I need to wake up.

Too much imagination.

Too much brandy soaked baked apple and ice cream on top of too much lemony chicken and caramelized onions.

Taylor struggled to run, to put her arms over her head to shield herself from the whizzing knives and the falling stacks of paper money. Her legs wouldn't move, her arms were trapped at her sides. Panic gripped her.

No!!!!

Think!

149

Chris and the blankets are holding you down.
Right.

Half awake, knowing where she was, feeling the warm presence of the soundly slumbering man, feeling safe, Taylor turned partially onto her side, snuggled closer to her husband's body and breathed in the scent of him. Dreams came again, contented happy dreams.

When the early morning light came to wake her Taylor drifted slowly from sleep to awareness. Tight against Chris's side she stayed quiet not wanting to wake him as she reviewed what she could remember of the morning eight days before when she had taken a bicycle ride after breakfast.

Sausages, French toast and chunky cherry jam.
Chris thought Laszlo was sleeping in.
You were going to go for a walk.
Marta told you about the bicycle.
Why had Chris, Lars, and Laszlo still been at the chateau?
The bankers were meeting with their lawyers.
Marta used a rag to wipe off the bike.
The tires were a little low — it was hard to pump on the gravel.
It was a beautiful day, blue sky, the green zucchini fields, distant trees, the vineyards with the tight tendrils of vines.
You were going to go as far as the other chateau.
I never got there.
Could have been on your way back.
No, I never got there.
There was the black car.
The dark-haired man in the black car.
Laszlo?
Maybe.
He looked surprised to see you.
Was he captive?
Did they have a gun on him?
A knife in his ribs?
The car did hit me on purpose!

Taylor's eyes came open. She was wide-awake and no longer questioning the possibility, she was absolutely sure that the black sedan's driver had deliberately run her into the ditch.

"Chris. Darling wake up."

"Huh?" he mumbled and then opened one eye to look at her speculatively. "What?"

"It was a black sedan that put me in the ditch, the driver ran me off the road on purpose." Taylor waited for him to make the connection.

Both of Chris's eyebrows raised, he sat up and looked down at her. "That's got to mean..."

"That what I saw that has them so anxious, I must have seen before the cows and the body, before the bike ride, or on it."

"Well, that certainly narrows the possibilities. What else have you remembered?" Chris's hand had trailed across her middle and slipped up under her pajama top as they talked and there was an entirely different conversation going on between their bodies.

"Nothing, really. The man, the passenger in the front seat, I think he was familiar..." Chris turned her to him and leaned down to rain little kisses down her cheek. "...familiar looking, but..."

First things first.

Right you are.

Taylor gave herself up to the moment.

"Familiar you said?" Chris took up the conversation where they'd left off.

"Dark. Dark hair, dark eyes, handsome."

"Laszlo?!"

"I don't know," Taylor said slowly. "I can't make myself remember Laszlo. Not yet anyway. I remember where we met and how. I remember that he seemed dangerous, that he frightened me and that he saved me but I can't get his face in focus."

"Dangerous huh?" Chris' eyes twinkled, "And handsome."

"Hey sleepy heads, we have news!" The booming announcement from outside the door was accompanied by loud banging.

Chris was out of the bed in an instant, pulling his robe about him as he strode to the door leaving Taylor just enough time to get the disheveled covers tugged up to her chin before he flung it open.

"What? Have they found him? Is he OK?"

"It is good news," Lars said, stepping into the room his glowing cheeks and broad smile making him look even more Santa Claus than usual, "But not that good, I am afraid. Good morning, Taylor."

Taylor started to reply but Lars' news would not wait for a further polite exchange of pleasantries.

"Overnight, thanks to your CIA friends, our careful bankers have received sufficient proof of drug and terrorist connections to the accounts we have inquired about to agree, not only to freeze all of them, but to freeze several associated accounts we knew nothing of until such time as we either prove conclusively the paper trail, or agree to dismiss any claim for lack of evidence. It is more than we had hoped."

"But that's great." Chris said, pumping Lars hand.

"Most certainly," Lars agreed, " But..."

"It doesn't give us much time to find Laszlo," Chris said. "If he is still alive they'll be only too glad to take out some of their angst on him."

He began gathering clothes as he spoke.

"Taylor, me first for the shower. But don't be long. We're going to have to figure out what to do with you today."

"Hey," Taylor yelled to a door that was already closing. "I'm a big grown girl who..." the door clanked shut and she heard the two men's voices fade as they headed toward the stairs. "...can take care of herself."

152

Well, I can.

As long as those invisible men are out there, coughing in the shadows.

Paranoia argued with bravado while she made the bed and selected clothes for the day. She arrived at the bathroom door just as Chris was exiting. He was, she noticed, wearing a suit and looking very official. "What about our walk?"

"There will be time for that after breakfast. Our meeting's not 'til ten. They wanted time to get their records organized."

Marta stuck her head out the door. "Better hurry up. Adie's made muffins and I'm not sure Lars is going to be able to resist for long."

"Save me one," Taylor said. "I'll be right there."

There were still three on the plate when Taylor dropped her tote and sweater on the sofa and slid onto the bench in her now customary spot. Adie was nowhere to be seen, Marta was in the kitchen, head in the refrigerator and Chris had slid to the end of the bench, next to Lars, their heads bent over several sheets of paper covered with Lars' cryptic scrawl. Taylor poured herself a cup of coffee and reached for an oatmeal muffin full of nuts and dried blueberries. She slathered it with butter and then sighed in contentment with the first bite.

Must be a thousand calories.

Who's counting.

Good thing there's elastic in your waistband.

Taylor'd decided on her white slacks and red turtleneck, opting for sneakers instead of sandals. She picked an errant crumb from her chest and tried not to eavesdrop too obviously on what the men were saying, but found it impossible not to tune in when Bellas was mentioned.

"I don't know if he was too smart to lead us to his bosses or they were too smart to give him anything but a cell phone number," Lars said.

"Let's have him picked up on the forged passport charge," Chris suggested. "That should get him out of the picture long enough for us to finish our business. At least the people gunning for Taylor will be amateurs. It should take two or even three days for them to get another professional."

"If I read what's gone down this morning right, another twenty-four hours, forty-eight maximum, and your part," Lars paused, "your and Laszlo's part of this will be over and it will be left to me to wrap up which agencies of which governments can lay claim to the funds. I suspect the bankers are counting on getting back their legal fees and perhaps a percentage in appreciation for their cooperation. I will make them work for it."

"My part's not over until we know for sure what happened to Laszlo," Chris vowed. "If I thought for one minute she'd let me, I'd send Taylor home under armed guard."

"I heard that," Taylor said, reaching for a second muffin. "I'm not going anywhere without you. Though I will admit to being in serious danger of blowing my cholesterol level to a new high. I remember more than enough about our life together to know we are always safer together than we are apart."

"That's arguable," Chris said, chuckling. "But in this instance, I agree. You won't be safe anywhere as long as they think there is something you know that we don't. So, finish stuffing your pretty face with Adie's killer muffins and we'll take that walk, work off some of the calories and maybe give your memory a boost."

"I shall make some calls and see to Bellas among other things."

Lars emptied the coffee carafe into his cup, added two heaping spoons of sugar and a generous pour of cream and pushed back his chair.

Despite the bright sun there was a sharpness to the air and Taylor was glad for her sweater. Morning dew glistened off the broad green leaves of the zucchini plants and sat like crystal beads in the golden blossoms. The gravel road looked darker, each damp stone a black jewel in the morning light.

"I've been wondering," Taylor said, "how do they know I haven't remembered? In fact, how do they know I lost my memory in the first place?"

"The doctor perhaps," Chris answered. "Marta may have mentioned it to the bread man, one of the policemen who came about the body or even Edward could have told any number of people. It wasn't any great secret at the time."

"And they snuck into the chateau, to be sure?"

"And to see what else they could hear or find."

"Like the phony lists you planted?"

Taylor slowed, eyeing the silent house in the vineyard. The shutters were still closed, no sign of habitation.

"Who do you suppose tends the vines?"

"Don't stare dear, you'll make the nice man with the binoculars and the gun nervous," Chris said, taking her elbow and moving her on. "Isn't this about where you went in the ditch?"

"Yes, you can still see the marks made by bicycle tires. What nice man? Our nice man with a gun or their nice man with a gun?"

"Our nice man with a gun. Their man would of course be considered a sneaking low life. If you open all the shutters ever so slightly they still looked closed but from the inside you can see everything, particularly from the second floor. They can watch the approach to the chateau from three sides at the same time."

"And the blind spot?" Taylor asked. She noted that bicycle tire marks in the soft verge confirmed she had been coming from the chateau when she'd veered suddenly into the ditch.

Too bad there had been no watchers in the house in the vineyard then.

"A pair of hardy souls cold camping in the trees in that tangle of a back garden. Now tell me again about the dark, handsome man in the black car. When did you see him?"

"After I got up out of the ditch. I was going to go that way, toward the other chateau. Then the car came out of the drive and I saw him when it passed me."

"Out of the drive? Are you sure? There's an intersection just before the chateau, might he have come around the corner?"

"I... yes, I suppose so." Taylor couldn't see the corner clearly from where she was standing. She only knew she had seen the black car turn toward her. "The car that hit me, or tried to, it came from the other direction. I guess they could have made a loop and come back to see..."

If you were hurt?

If you were dead.

"What I don't understand is why they didn't finish the job right then?" Chris pondered.

He'd taken her hand and they were strolling on toward the trees, the distant chateau and the still hidden corner.

"Base inefficiency," Taylor offered.

"So it would seem," Chris agreed. "And, the facts imply that, whatever you saw, it was after you left the drive on the bicycle and before you were run down."

"But there's nothing there," Taylor said. "The road down to the river edge, the zucchini fields, the river bank, the vineyard, nothing unusual and no one. At least I don't think I saw anyone. Ohh... I don't remember, Chris. I just don't remember that part at all. The time right before and right after I woke up in the ditch — it's all still so fuzzy. I have no idea how much I really remember, or have surmised or just plain made up to fill in blank spots."

They were closing on the corner and Taylor could see the intersection, a sharp left turn between giant trees. Three trees farther on there was another sharp left between stone pillars, a driveway closed to general access by formidable wrought iron gates. As they drew nearer she could see the gates had received a recent coat of dark green paint, the swirled spires at the top tip ends gilded. The chateau behind the gates was eerily similar to Adie and Marta's home but in much better repair. The gardens were neat and formal, no boarded up windows, a whole fleet of black sedans in the drive.

"What Edward is lusting after," Taylor observed.

"Impressive," Chris agreed. "But not as charming as its twin."

"You're a romantic."

"Romantic or otherwise, I'm about to be late. We'd better get back."

CHAPTER 24

Leaving stern orders to stick to the chateau, showing herself hourly on the porch or in the front garden so the men in the house in the vineyard would be able to see her, Chris hugged Taylor and departed with Lars. Since she wasn't sure if Marta or Adie knew the extent of the situation, Taylor pleaded headache when Marta invited her to accompany her grocery shopping. Despite Chris's orders she'd felt inclined to go.

She'll need help carrying packages.

I'll get another look at the goodies in a Swiss deli section.

And your little entourage? How are they going to manage?

They kept up in Italy.

They knew ahead in Italy and Chris was with you.

Party pooper.

Selfish brat.

It's not fair to leave Marta with all the work.

It's not fair to put Marta, and perhaps others, in danger.

Dumb to make too easy a target of yourself.

Feeling only a little like she was giving in to paranoia Taylor accepted the Advil Marta offered and waved good-by from the porch, turning to glower briefly in the direction of the vineyard before taking the stairs to the second floor to get her book. Exiting her room, Taylor considered a side trip through Marta's apartment for a peek out the back at the copse of tall trees that sheltered the other pair of watchdogs.

You'll be seen, Lars will know even if Marta never does.

I'm not snooping into Lars or Marta's private things.

You're bored.

I'm curious.

Foolish.

Chris has barely left and you've plotted defiance twice.

"Oh for Pete's sake," Taylor sighed and went down the stairs and back to the great room. Adie was nowhere to be seen.

Taylor curled up on the window bench, fat pillows tucked behind her back, and tried to read. There was a heavy silence in the room; the only sound the ticking of a clock. A sudden humming startled her, bringing Taylor to her feet. It took scant seconds to identify the refrigerator as the source, but it was long enough to have sent her heart pounding.

"It's chilly in here," her voice seemed both too small and too loud in her own ears.

Taylor sat down and started her stress exercises, regulating her breathing, preaching calming thoughts to a reluctant and argumentative audience.

When Adie entered the room half an hour later she found Taylor deep in her book. "You are feeling better?"

"I feel fine. A little bored and wishing I'd gone with Marta after all but..."

"But there are things going on that would make that unwise," Adie said, coming to sit on the sofa. "It would be hard not to notice. Marta and I are quite aware that Lars and Christopher have very serious business to conduct. Always when Lars visits it is so. He never says, just goes off to his meetings and comes back to eat and tell stories about his youth and his wife and children and laugh. We know."

Adie pulled a tapestry tote from under the small table and took out her knitting.

"I am making Edward socks for Christmas. I make him two pair every year. His wife makes him three. He is very hard on his socks and he refuses to wear them if they have been darned."

"I can knit," Taylor said, surprised by the knowledge. "I made fancy Christmas stockings once. The kind American children hang on the mantle on Christmas Eve. They were darling. They were also entirely too large and stretchy. My husband – my ex-husband, the father of my children – always complained about how much it took to fill them."

159

You could have gone the rest of your life and not regretted forgetting him.

Be nice.

Without him I might not have had the stress or the bad heart.

Without him you would not have the children.

Or the grandchildren.

Or perhaps even Chris.

That much credit he does not get!

"Mother used to make a little bundle, generally a new handkerchief, with an orange and some hard candy. Edward and Peter got tin soldiers, one, sometimes two. The girls generally got ribbons. Ribbons for our braids. And they would be on the table waiting for us Christmas morning. There were Christmases with bigger presents in later years but to me, now, those bundles were the best presents ever."

"Adie what do you know about the other chateau, the one up the road? I know it was built at about the same time as this one. Chris and I walked there this morning. It's very similar, your tower is round and theirs is square but otherwise the buildings look very much alike."

"A brother or a cousin, a family member at any rate of the family who built this," Adie waved her knitting, the red sock with navy and white squares on its neck fluttered like a flag. "It was a local tale that they were so afraid of bandits, even in going that short distance that they had a tunnel built between the two, connecting the basements. It is very possible they feared the serfs that farmed the fields, they're said to have treated them very badly. When they placed the town's new sewer outfall in the road, the one that comes in just before you get to the other chateau, Edward claims they found the caved-in passage. But as children we were all over this basement and never found any sign of a door or an entrance to a tunnel, I don't think there was one. It, the other chateau, was in much worse condition for a long time. Then a wealthy man bought it."

"And gave Edward ideas?" Taylor asked.

"So it would seem," Adie sighed. "It is only that Edward can be so determined when he gets an idea in his head. Persistence can be a good trait - and a bad one. Marta says these socks are too bright. Do you think Edward will like them?"

"I think they're beautiful. Adie," Taylor began, a curious thought tickling at her to ask, "Did Petra ever get lavender ribbons for Christmas?"

"Lavender? No, I got red ones, Petra got blue, Marta yellow, and Elsbeth pink. It was the same every year. Why?"

"Nothing, it's silly. I had a dream, about a girl with long braids and lavender ribbons."

"Perhaps I should cancel my lunch appointment," Adie said. "You should not be alone."

"Nonsense. I have my book and more up in the room if I finish this one. I think I might sit out in the garden awhile, probably catch a nap in the sun like the other day."

Adie eyed Taylor seriously, as if measuring her health and stability. "Very well. Marta has left you some lunch in the refrigerator and there is a jug of lemonade. The bread is under the white cloth by the stove and the cookies are in mother's sugar crock — the big one with blue stripes."

That settled, Adie bent her attention to the turning of the heel of Edward's sock.

Mindful of Chris's orders Taylor went to stand briefly on the porch and then returned to her book.

Just before noon Adie departed and Taylor began to prepare for an al fresco afternoon. She checked the cushion on the lounge in the garden, sun-warmed, morning dew long dried and gone, she shook it to dislodge any spiders or bugs, then brought out the pair of pillows from the window seat and the throw from the sofa. Taylor entered the kitchen on tiptoe, permission or not it seemed like a forbidden act. A tray was on the counter set with a red placemat, matching napkin, a tall glass and silver. The refrigerator along with the carafe of lemonade yielded a yellow plate, its daisy pattern obscured by several slices of chicken breast, a salad of rice, green peas, celery, and walnuts and a generous wedge of brie. The niche in the door of the refrigerator chunked cubes of ice into her glass, just like at home. Taylor cut herself a slab of bread and, mindful of the story of Petra and the soup tureen, with great care secured a handful of what her mother had called butterscotch brownies. The tray was loaded and it took an additional trip into the house to retrieve her book.

Like a queen, Taylor thought settling on the lounge. *Or at least a lady of privilege.*

Very fitting.

What about the nice men with the guns?

Wonder if they packed a sandwich, they can hardly order in.

Such a good girl — right out here where they can see you every minute.

Right out here where the bad guys can see you.

Hope that our side doesn't take a nap after lunch, too.

She couldn't resist lifting her glass in salute to her unseen companions.

CHAPTER 25

Taylor cleaned her plate, finished the cookies and half of the lemonade, then barely managed to read three pages before drifting off. When she woke the ice had melted in her glass and a small brown bird sat on the edge of the tray pecking at the cookie crumbs.

"Well, hello there."

The bird did not take flight though it did take time from its gleaning to look at her speculatively. Deciding she seemed reasonably inert, the bird continued its feasting. Taylor watched from between lowered lashes until, full, or out of crumbs, the bird launched suddenly and disappeared into the trees that shaded the drive. The bird's flight drew her eye up and a movement on the second story balcony near the door to her room caught her attention. Taylor sat up, flinging back the robe, the paperback slid to the ground. On her feet, hands on hips, she scanned the balcony. There was nothing — no one.

They're in the chateau again!

Your imagination.

Julius, sunning himself on the balcony railing.

A bird.

YOUR IMAGINATION!!!

More curious than careful, Taylor made for the stairs. There was no one on the balcony, Marta's door was closed and locked, the tower room above the bathroom was empty as was her bedroom. The door to the other bedroom was locked and the corridor that led to the steps to the third floor was empty. Taylor entered the narrow passage, trying the arched door as well as the one on the landing, finding them locked as well. There seemed to be no additional disturbance in the dust on the stairs. Every interior voice sided with the paranoid naysayer within and still she climbed the steps. There was no one in view of the

163

lady with the water jug. There was no one, not even Julius to be seen in the great space above the bedrooms. Previous explorations had overlaid so many prints in the dust that a dozen new ones would not have been noticeable. She found Julius in the center of the door to his room, cleaning his paws.

"Was that you?"

Julius looked up and then continued his grooming.

"Sorry for the intrusion," Taylor told him. Having come this far she could not resist crossing to the back corner thinking there could be no harm in slipping down through Marta's laundry room for a quick check of the back garden. She found Julius's water dish full. That door, too, was locked.

Her heart had been pounding with excitement — with fear — with expectation.

Don't you feel foolish?

Had to have been Julius.

Bet you got the guys watching from the vineyard all excited.

Taylor made haste back to the garden to show herself. She was wide-awake. Retrieving the book from the path she read a few pages and then lost interest.

Julius?

A shadow?

A bird?

Was it big enough to be a person?

It was moving from our bedroom door toward the passage to the third floor stairs.

Back to Julius.

Back to a person.

You didn't check the dark corners that carefully. There could have been a small army hidden up there.

Good guy coming to check on me?

Bad guy coming to check you out, permanently.

Good guys would have seen him.

Good guy, bad guy, how'd he get in?

How'd he get out?

He's here. Behind a locked door.
In a dark corner.
He could have come down the stairs and hid in the
bathroom.

"Stop it," Taylor said sternly.

She took a deep calming breath, marked her place in the book, and took her tray in.

Feeling safer in plain view than within the chateau's stone walls, Taylor was back in the garden, book in her lap, pondering the puzzle when Marta arrived in a taxi, the trunk full of groceries. By the time the groceries were all in and away Adie had also returned.

The day had lost its brightness, the shadows lengthening when Chris called to say he and Lars would be another hour or more.

"Problems?" Taylor asked.

"Quite the opposite," Chris said. "It's as if we had pulled the little Dutch boy's finger from the dike and the information is flooding out. I think, once convinced of the illegal source of the funds, the idea of supporting drug dealers and terrorist's anonymity, more particularly the idea of the world press letting it be known they'd done so, outweighed any concerns of client privilege or privacy. We need to listen for as long as they want to talk."

"I certainly agree. I can wait for my dinner if Lars can."

"And you're safe. They have night-vision glasses," Chris said, precluding her question about the coming of dark.

"And Adie will be home, in her apartment," Taylor said.

What's an ancient if somewhat daunting Swiss miss going to do? Throw cheeses at the bad guys?

Whatever's necessary. I wouldn't want to get on her bad side.

165

Maybe...

Taylor wasn't totally convinced no matter how reassuring she'd tried to sound.

Better than being in the chateau all alone.

Laszlo disappeared with Chris and Lars here.

Alone is fine. It's the makers of all those other footprints that have me concerned.

"I'll see you when you get here," Taylor said, trying to keep her voice light.

Dusk had truly fallen when Marta left for Elsbeth's. Adie had already retreated to prepare for her young guest. Taylor, feeling vulnerable, turned on all the lights and gave up the window seat for the sofa. Unable to concentrate on her book she explored the room and found several magazines in a magazine rack tucked behind the overstuffed chair, all in Italian. Looking at the pictures, using her so-so Spanish as a springboard to the Italian sub-titles Taylor pieced together the story of the restoration of one of those part barn, part living space huts that seemed to be everywhere. This one was wood, giant, squared-off whole trees stacked much like American log houses into the typical Swiss structure. It was in the village of Zermatt, a ski resort where cars were left in a parking lot at the edge of town, even delivery vehicles forbidden on the streets with the exception of a few weeks in summer.

Chris told me about Zermatt — we were going to go there.

On a train you drive your car onto.

Another memory accounted for — now remember the rest.

Rest of what.

The bike ride.

Taylor tried, she concentrated on that morning. Breakfast. The bike. Wobbling like she had when she first learned to ride and then the exhilaration as the ease of balance came back and she was whizzing along the dirt road.

But what did you see?

The road.

Trees.
Zucchini plants.
Grapevines.
Do you know that or are you guessing because that's what you've seen since?
Did you see the black car that hit you? Where did it come from?
Behind me!
I heard it behind me. I looked over my shoulder. It was a black car, like our rental. At first I thought it was Chris coming after me for some reason. Then I tried to get to the edge of the road — out of the way so it could pass. It hit my handlebar.
An accident?!
I don't think so.
So now you're back to why.
Meanness?
You mean for no reason at all!
Doesn't jive with what happened after. The blond that splatted in the courtyard at the museum and Bellas with his knife were not out to kill you just for the fun of it.

"Laszlo!" Taylor said to the vast, empty room. The word echoed slightly in her ears.

Did you see Laszlo that morning even if no one else did?

There was total silence for her otherwise vocal inner chorus.

All right, did he tell you something, the night before perhaps?
Were you alone, even for a few minutes?
Think.
Bellas could not have come cheap.
What you know... what they think you know, was worth the risk taken by the two at the museum.

167

Worth sneaking around the dark and dangerous top story of this semi-crumbling ruin and peeking through holes in floors.

That had to do with Chris and Lars' work.

Your point is?

Maybe wanting to kill me has nothing to do with what they are up to.

Unlikely.

Possible.

Unlikely.

Where did Marta leave that Advil?

CHAPTER 26

The Advil, Taylor remembered, had been returned to a cupboard in the kitchen. Rather than intrude again on forbidden territory, this time without an invitation, she opted to go up to her bedroom for her own supply.

The light from the balcony splayed across the floor of the bedroom and sent an eerie chill up Taylor's back. She fumbled her hand across the wall seeking and then finding the knobby protrusion of the light switch. With a click a new set of shadows danced across the broad planks of the floor. Puddles of light from the bedside lamps lit the jewel tones of the many carpets and made glitter of the fine dust on the wood surfaces. Her tote lay on the bed still fat with the pajamas she'd stuffed in it after her shower. She pulled out the T-top to facilitate her search for the familiar round bottle and found what she wanted. Taylor downed two tablets sans water. She was reaching into the tote for the silk pajama bottoms when she heard the now familiar sounds from above, a screeching and scampering.

Julius after his dinner.

There's dust on the bedroom floor!

Ask Marta where they keep the dust mop.

There were no footprints, no paw prints, no dust, on Julius's floor!

Sure there were. It's the light.

Taylor's hand bypassed the pajama bottoms and sought instead her penlight. Out of habit she slung the tote over her shoulder and headed for the door. It was necessary to switch on the penlight the minute she stepped into the corridor that led to the stairs. Familiar now with both the steps and the narrow strip of floor past the fresco, Taylor did not slow until she reached the space above the bedrooms. She flashed the thin beam around the walls and into the corners. This time she knew why

169

the piles of stone seemed so familiar, she had searched the tumbled interiors of Mayan ruins for Chris.

And you found him.

The knowledge gave her satisfaction and boosted her spirits. Still the deep shadows that gyrated as the shaft of light passed across pillars and piles of stone and boards got her full attention.

"Julius, where are you?" Taylor called softly.

Her heart was pounding then nearly stopped altogether as black cat, eyes blazing, arched up from behind a pile of rubble. It leapt through the shaft of light throwing a giant feline shadow across the floor that shrunk at her feet to the still formidable but less threatening real Julius.

"There you are," Taylor said, swallowing.

Julius sat looking up at her as if waiting for instructions. The screeching sound came again startling both of them. Julius rose and stalked off in the general direction of his room.

That confirms it. Julius is not responsible for that noise.
Do you really want to find out who — what — is?
It sounded like it came from the chateau, from the walls.
You should wait and tell Chris when he gets here.
Absolutely.

Wise course of action or no, Taylor followed the cat, swinging her light left and right.

It's no light saber.
It's not even a decent flashlight.
Better than no light.
Better, would be downstairs sitting on the sofa.

Julius was waiting for her in his room, sitting at the threshold.

"A welcome or a warning?"

Julius of course did not reply, nor did he move. Taylor stepped past him and moved her light around the bare walls, the floor and the ceiling and then the floor again.

Empty.
Duh.

170

Another wild goose chase.
There is dust on the floor.
But not much.
Not any more than the bedroom.
The bedroom gets cleaned regularly!

Upon closer examination Taylor saw dainty paw prints to and from the window and a clean spot where Julius lay to soak up the morning sun. She could also see a wide assortment of human footprints.

You brought Chris and Lars here.
That doesn't explain the floor being so clean.
Doesn't explain that either!

Taylor couldn't remember either Chris or Lars walking up to the wall at the left end of the room but there were prints, several sets, visible in the low, slanted beam of the penlight. More as she held the light nearer the floor.

"Curious," Taylor exclaimed and stepped past Julius to examine closer the floor next to the wall.

"Meowww!" Julius scolded and came to stand between her and the wall, sitting down on the prints she was trying to read. Taylor ran the beam back and forth from the wall to the door, trying to make sense of what she was seeing.

Not much of a great white hunter.
Leave it for Chris and Lars.

Deciding to do just that Taylor reached down to give Julius a pat. Standing as close to the wall as she was her derrière bumped it as she bent over.

Damn, bet I got a mark on my white pants.
The wall gave!
It gave, I felt it.

And it was still giving. There was no time to step away from the wall, with a screech — "the screech" — the wall swung away behind her. Caught by surprise Taylor lost her balance, falling backward into the moving wall. Julius let out a yowl — Taylor had no time to yell. She braced, expecting a momentary connection to the floor she instead found herself airborne.

What!!!

There was an instant of contact with some metal object that fell away from her as she continued downward, sliding down its length. The penlight, tight in a hand she clutched tighter for fear of losing her light source, flashed its beam across stone walls, broken wood beams and what looked for all the world like an aluminum ladder. With a thud that knocked the breath from her body and sent sharp pains shooting in all directions Taylor landed on her back. The beam from the penlight was pointed straight up, a dozen feet or more above she saw Julius, eyes reflecting the light. She lay still, trying to breathe, trying, without moving, to inventory the condition of her body.

Everything hurts.

Breathe!

Nothing hurts bad enough to be broken.

The white pants are wiped out.

What's the lump under my shoulder?

Your tote.

"Emphhhuh," Taylor sputtered, trying to sit up.

The first place she tried to put her hand for support there was no there there. A quick inspection with the penlight showed she was on a platform in a stone and wood walled shaft, a kind of landing, though no stairs went up or down. A few inches farther left and she'd have been falling still. Above her there was another yowl from Julius followed by the screech, the sound of the secret door closing. A chilling bit of knowledge quickly confirmed when her light caught the door as it settled into place with a slight grating sound.

"Now what?"

It sounded too loud and Taylor was fearful of who might hear.

Someone came this way minutes ago!

Yeah, but they used the ladder.

Use the ladder and leave.
Right.
Taylor checked the perimeter of the landing and noted that the ladder had fallen sidewise, one side off into space and lodged at an angle. She put the penlight in her mouth and tugged at the ladder with both hands.
Stuck tight.
Your weight wedged it in.
The ladder saved you from a longer drop.
Climb it anyway.
What if it falls?
Then it won't be stuck anymore.
Very funny.
Clutching the penlight, Taylor climbed the ladder placing her foot in the V formed by the step and the side, hanging on as best she could with a hand and a wrist to work with. When she got to the top she found she was several feet below and far to the side of where she would need to stand to reach the metal ring hanging so mockingly from the inside of the secret panel.
If you can't go up, go down.
This is how they get into the chateau.
How they took the papers.
How they took Laszlo!
How the sneaks came to look through the hole in the ceiling.
So there has to be another way into — and out of — this shaft.
Clever girl.
Very logical.
Dangerous!
Not exactly safe to stay here.
The internal argument settled and again on the more or less firm footing of the landing, Taylor gave a serious inspection to her situation. Wooden stairs had once wound up the shaft but the landing she was on and the one

below it were no longer connected. Only splintered wood remained of the landing at the very top, behind the secret panel. Moving her light across the ancient timbers she now stood on, her heart leapt with the sight of a dark arc cut deep in the wood, but more importantly, signs the dust had been moved recently. Taylor ran the light over the wooden wall behind the arc, looking for an iron ring, and finding none. She did find the massive iron hinges and signs they had been oiled in the not too distant past.

A lever then.

A mental walk through the chateau and Taylor was convinced that Marta's guestroom — Laszlo's room — was on the other side of the wall if only she could figure out how it opened.

They got it open.

They took Laszlo out.

The ring should be right about...

"...here." There was a hole, a piece of the wood chipped away - recently from the looks of it - the ring broken out and missing. No matter how Taylor tried she could not get purchase enough to move the door. "Now what?" Taylor pointed her light into the void beneath the landing.

The top of another aluminum ladder, a mere rectangle, four inches by a bit more than a foot long glinted back at her from at least a foot down.

This is going to be fun.

Don't knock it over too.

Don't do this.

What, I should sit here and scream?

No one would hear you.

My point exactly.

"When I get home — If I get home — I am never going farther than the grocery store, ever again."

With a sigh for the fate of her white pants and a small groan to acknowledge her protesting body, Taylor got to her knees and backed over the edge of the landing, dangling a leg until it made contact with the top of the ladder. She felt the ladder move away from her, heart in her throat she steadied it, then slid the foot past the top, downward to the next rung clutching the dirty wood of the landing with her upper body. Both feet found the rung and she pushed herself more upright and panned the light briefly around the ladder and the space below.

You thought maybe the rung was levitating in space?

Taylor began to descend, gathering confidence with each downward step.

First floor, everybody out.

This landing was new wood, dirty from passing traffic but not from time. At one end a black hole loomed, an aluminum ladder waited below. The walls bore no marks of inwardly swinging panels. Not daunted, Taylor looked carefully for signs of some other kind of door. There were no hinges, no ring, no clue that it was now or had ever been an access point. There was, however, a knothole in the wood wall and Taylor tried to peer through into the total darkness. Even when she held the penlight to the hole there wasn't much to see.

Coats, clothes. It's the back of Piet's closet!

Taylor spent several minutes pushing and tugging at various boards to no avail.

He probably unknowingly blocked it when he redid things.

Taylor had a mental image of a shelf over the closet bar holding her prisoner.

Onward and downward.

Repeating her prior movements, Taylor lowered herself off the edge of the landing. Feeling splinters from the new wood snag at her red turtleneck, she mourned its fortune.

Focus.

You can buy a new shirt.

175

Taylor climbed down to the basement level fully expecting to find herself in a tunnel. "Another landing?!" Stone walls on all sides and absolutely no sign of hinges, a ring, latch or lever.

Another new landing!

This wasn't done in a night. Somebody knew ahead of time we'd be here – Chris and Lars and Laszlo would be here.

Laszlo is a double agent?

Doesn't feel right.

Lars is a double agent?!

Well, it sure isn't Chris.

What do you really remember about any of them?

Oh, come on now...

Taylor lowered herself off the wooden platform, no longer thinking about her once white pants or the shredded red turtleneck shirt, adrenaline pumping too hard to feel her aches and pains.

A sub-basement!

That's why the children never found a tunnel.

Probably comes out just beyond the trees or the middle of the zucchini fields...

Or in the other chateau?

Marta said Edward said they found the tunnel collapsed.

Marta said there was no tunnel.

Good point.

"Guess I'm going to find out." The ladder stood on a new wood floor and for a minute Taylor thought it was one more landing and she would have to go deeper yet. Under the ladder she spotted the ring missing from the second floor. Playing her penlight around her position she found she was on a kind of dais, a raised platform in a middle of a moderate sized pillared room that belled out from the bottom of the stairwell. To her left and right the walls were adorned with frescos akin in style to the lady with the water jug on the third floor. The other two walls had several niches — three to each side of dark openings one of which had to be the fabled tunnel. In the niches were carved stone caskets.

"The family mausoleum! Makes a kind of sense. Now which way?"

Turned around and tired, Taylor swung the light from one end of the room to the other and then went right, she could tell at once she was in an additional burial chamber. Niches lined the walls three high in some places. In others, small alcoves held ornate caskets.

How'd they get all that marble and statuary down here?

She hurried onward not entirely comfortable with her surroundings, moving the light constantly, looking for steps or a door. Not far along the passage she came to a halt.

"Dead end."

She laughed nervously at the bad joke. Ahead of her was the largest of the tombs, ornately carved pillars decorated the entrance and a stone bench sat at the foot of a marble casket on a cherub decorated base. Taylor was about to turn and try the other direction when her light caught a hint of blue on the floor behind the bench.

Don't have time to sight see.

Only take a second.

Taylor turned the light full down into the space between the bench and the marble cherubs. "Oh..." she drew in a deep breath. "Hello Petra."

A blue bow adorned a pile of birdlike bones - a second bow could be seen sticking from beneath an obviously human skull. Taylor knew she should be shocked, maybe even frightened but she also knew the little girl had been here a very long time and those that loved her would be glad for her to be found at last.

Presuming you ever get the chance to tell them.

You don't find the way out you'll be joining her.

"Exit has to be the other way," Taylor decided aloud. "Someone will be back for you soon, Petra, I promise." She retraced her steps, noting as she passed through the room at the bottom of the stairwell that, had she but paid attention, the scuffing of dust on the floor would have shown her the way the first time. No niches here, a half-dozen steps into the passage there were three stone steps down and then she passed through the remnants of a wooden door down two more steps and into a low arched tunnel.

Barely wide enough for a casket to pass.
Those ancient Italians must have been small men.
Chris would have to stoop.
Lars would get stuck!

CHAPTER 27

Taylor was a considerable way into the tunnel before it occurred to her that there was absolutely nowhere to hide.

You'll hear them coming.

They'll hear you running.

I'm wearing sneakers.

You pant like a freight train.

She stopped and listened. There was no sound but her own thudding heart. She flashed her light forward, the tunnel walls continued straight as far as a pair of AA batteries could reach.

Don't stop now, if it comes out at the other chateau you have almost a mile to go.

The air was still, musty, Taylor kept her thoughts from the probability of four-legged residents. Striding as purposefully forward as she could under the circumstances she couldn't help wonder exactly how Petra had died.

Fell through the wall, just like you.

She didn't have a ladder to deflect her onto the landing.

She didn't have a light.

How did she find the tomb?

Was it some injury from the fall that killed her?

What must she have thought of the cherubs when she felt them!

Perhaps she thought she was dead and this was heaven.

She knows better now.

The narrow beam, bouncing along in the blackness that both followed and preceded her, cut across a deep shadow ahead on the left. With quickening steps Taylor rushed forward, not the least sure of what she was going to find, or what she might be able to do, but more than ready to end her walk in the claustrophobic passage under the zucchini fields.

"Damn!" The word echoed down the stone corridor and Taylor hoped she had not caused some pure hearted Italian lady in repose behind her to roll over. No steps or even a side passage — just an alcove with a bench. The wall above the bench was adorned with a mosaic — heavily laden grapevines coiled around a scene of snowcapped mountains.

It was tempting to sit awhile but a sense of urgency pushed her onward.

You sit down it's going to hurt to get up.
Find them before they find you.
Find Laszlo before they kill him.
Find a way out of here before the dark and walls get to you.
Always good to have a plan.

The next break in the tunnel's walls was on the right, another alcove and bench. The mosaic above this one depicted a lake among rolling hills and was ringed with pink roses. Taylor touched the surface of a rose petal and realized the wall had been recently cleaned.

An aesthetically sensitive terrorist?!!

Several yards farther on Taylor made another startling discovery. The floor was ramping, very slightly, and angling off to the left. As a result when she pointed her light ahead it hit the wall of the tunnel just below the arch of the ceiling.

"Wires!" Taylor followed the wires back toward her with the beam and soon discovered a light fixture, a neon bar much like the ones under her kitchen counters. The wires continued into the darkness behind her. "Lights. They've wired it for lights!"

Not a last minute kind of thing to do.
Were there lights in the catacomb?
In the stairwell?
You didn't look.

How long have they been playing fun and games - peeking at people in the chateau?

What interest could Marta and Adie possibly hold for a bunch of drug connected, money laundering, terrorism supporters?

Finding out how they got in sure hasn't made the why of it any clearer.

Could be the great interest in seeing you dead has to do with something you saw inside the chateau before your bike ride.

Did you see something strange in the chateau?

Such as...?

Don't remember.

If you remembered we wouldn't be in this mess.

"Wonder where the light switch is?"

At the bad guys' end of the tunnel.

Taylor had come to a third bench, on her left. The mosaic was again ringed in grapes, this time the scene was one of a sunlit patio filled with pots of bright flowers.

Windows.

Outdoor views to help those who passed feel less confined.

Imagine this tunnel with only flickering candles.

Medieval.

Probably looks like a subway station with the lights on.

Better hope they don't go on, it's a long way back and they couldn't help but see you.

Need a little positive thinking here.

I'm positive if those lights go on you're dead meat.

The downward slope had flattened out and the tunnel was running arrow straight. The benches had apparently divided the distance in quarters. Now when Taylor flashed her mini beam ahead she could see a difference at the end of the light's reach.

A door.

Without it there would probably be a cold wind blowing through here.

What if it's locked?

Find out before you start worrying.

Every step brought her nearer to the door that blocked her progress. And with every step Taylor felt her sense of urgency turning to outright panic. Her heart was racing, her palms sweaty.

Not helping.

Calm thoughts.

Don't have any calm thoughts.

The door was a new one, a duplicate no doubt of the original, heavy planks were bolted together and mounted on sturdy hinges. The latch was visible from several yards. When she reached it at last Taylor could see no sign of a lock.

Don't!!! A major portion of the inner chorus bellowed as she reached to open the door.

How do you know there isn't someone on the other side?

Can't just stand here.

Can't go back.

Have to go ahead.

Not enough choices.

No good ones.

Taylor put a hand on the wrought iron latch but couldn't bring herself to apply the pressure it would take to lift it. She lay her head against the door, listening and hearing nothing.

Silly.

It's too thick.

Get on with it.

She took in a long, deep breath and held it as she pressed ever so lightly and felt, more than heard, the latch lift. A second deep breath and she turned off the penlight and slipped it into the side pocket of her tote, then, free hand against the stone jamb, eased the door forward watching for a crack of light, listening for a sound.

CHAPTER 28

It was dim, but not dark on the other side of the door. Taylor found herself in a short passage, the twin to the one at the other end of the tunnel. A faint glow, like a night-light, was evident, coming from the room she was sure was the bottom of a corresponding secret staircase. Creeping on tiptoe she covered the distance to the entrance.

"A carbon copy," Taylor whispered.

Well, almost.

There were niches complete with marble encased occupants on either side of where she stood. The walls to her right and left were covered with frescos, much more religious in nature than the ones at the other end. Directly across the pillared hall, behind the ornately carved bottom landing of the expected staircase, Taylor saw another wall of six niches with a paneled door in its middle. For a moment the medieval atmosphere prevailed, it was hard to believe she had not slipped back several centuries. Only the gray metal box with four very modern looking light switches on its face about shoulder height on the wall just inside the passage said Twenty-first Century. The dim light floated down from the stairwell.

Now what?

Find Laszlo.

What makes you think he's still here?

Find a way out of here and let Chris and Lars come look for Laszlo.

A better idea.

Male voices echoed down the stairs and started Taylor considering a whole new set of problems.

Hide!

Where?

"I tell you, she was talking to someone. A man, she called him Julius."

The speaker had a high whiny voice.

"You had a gun."

The other man had an accent Taylor did not recognize.

"It's dark up there. I could have missed," the whiner alibied.

"Could have gotten yourself shot you mean. Coward!" The man with the accent continued to speak, cussing the whiner out from the tone of what was said in a language that was as unintelligible to her as his accent.

Knowing there was no exit behind her, Taylor made for the door across the room hoping against hope that it led to another passage of tombs and that the two men were not on their way down to pay their respects to the dearly departed.

Ninny, what if the door's locked, pessimism yelped half way across the room. Taylor was circling wide around the stairs in an effort to stay out of the sight of those descending.

Too late now.

No other choice.

Please, let it be unlocked.

Please, don't let it squeak.

It was and it didn't. Taylor quickly closed the door behind her, holding her breath as the heavy latch engaged with the tiniest of clicks, and she was at once alone in absolute dark. Still holding the handle, her head against the solid panel she listened and heard, or thought she heard, the two men continue to converse. Afraid to move, not sure what she might bump into and signal her presence, afraid not to move lest they come her way, heart racing and a dull ache threatening to spread across her chest Taylor closed her eyes to the darkness and began her series of calming mental exercises. Eventually her heart slowed, the ache in her chest retreated into relative par with the aches from the fall, and silence seemed to reign on the other side of the door.

No light gets in so none will get out.

Let's see where we are.

In a mausoleum.

She fumbled for the penlight and switched it on.

In a church!

Chapel.

Whatever.

It was exquisite. Taylor had no idea what century, but the silver candle holders and altar pieces, the white marble statues in gilded niches on either side, the carved pews all looked so right, so ready and waiting through the ages, she felt safe.

A sanctuary.

Not if the fellow who restored it finds you here.

Can't stay here.

Voices are gone.

Switching her light off, Taylor slowly, carefully, eased the door open. With the first crack, light poured in. The stairwell was flooded in light. And, she saw, so was the passage to the tunnel and the tunnel itself.

"If they've gone across to the chateau to find me..." she said, more moving her lips than speaking aloud.

Then now is a good time to see what's up the stairs.

To get out of here and get home.

What? In time to greet them at the other end?

Maybe — with the help of our friends from the house in the vineyard.

Maybe.

Just get out of here will you.

Taylor shut the chapel door and moving out of line of sight of the tunnel entrance as fast (and as quietly) as she could, circled to peek down the passage.

They're already past the rise and bend and out of sight.

Or they didn't go and are upstairs waiting for you.

Then why turn on the light.

Maybe only Whiny went.

Grumpy wouldn't have trusted him alone again.

"Hmmmmhuh," Taylor sighed, and turned toward the stairs.

It was sturdy, elegant even. Nicer than the one at the other end ever was she suspected, certainly what was left of it had been rough with no remnants of fine banisters or carpeting. Taylor took a final glance in the direction of the tunnel and started up. The steps turned and turned and turned again around an open center rectangle before she reached the first landing and Taylor wondered if she'd reached the basement, or as at the other end, passed it by.

The door was obvious, dark wood, not so nicely paneled as the chapel door. It was also locked. Taylor resisted the temptation to rattle the handle.

Two floors, possibly three, to go.

What if they're all locked?

What if Grumpy and Whiny come back and find you on the stairs?

If the doors are all locked they're going to find you eventually.

Stop with all the cheerful thinking.

Taylor had reached the next landing. There was another dark paneled door, with a shiny brass handle that turned with a gentle click. Restraining the urge to flee at once into and across the room beyond in search of the nearest outside door Taylor edged the door farther open. It was a library, the dark paneled shelves, roaring fire, leather chairs, and Persian rug kind of library that one thinks of as existing only in English manor houses.

And Swiss chateaux.

My, yes.

There was a stone step down to the library floor and Taylor had just advanced her foot to its center when she heard the television or perhaps it was a radio, for certain it was an American news report. Taylor pulled back into the stairwell leaving the door barely ajar and listened. She couldn't hear anything but the reporter and then the beginning of a commercial, the sound came from her right, from the same open arch that had appeared on her cursory inspection to be the only exit from the room. The view out the windows at the far end of the big room told her she was on the ground floor.

Two floors to go.

Taylor eased the door shut and, with a quick look down to be sure she was still alone, started up the next flight. The stairwell narrowed, no longer taking turns around a central opening, it coiled tightly over itself. A frosted bulb in a brass wall sconce centered on each wall above each run of steps cast a soft glow.

Too much light.

Better than climbing down ladders in the dark.

No place to hide.

If you don't want to sneak past some guy watching the news on the first floor just how do you propose to get back past him from the second or third?

Outside stairs, like Marta's.

Maybe.

What was that?

Alert for sounds, she heard a slight regular thudding but it was impossible to tell as it echoed in the stone shaft if it came from below or above her.

Someone coming up the stairs?

Whiny and Grumpy back so soon?

Someone coming down then?

Taylor peered above her with alarm but could see no farther than the next two runs of steps. There was, she noted again, no place to hide and kept climbing. Turning the next corner she could see the second floor landing. There was no door, a small new panic piled in on top of the knot of tension already gripping her.

There's a ring in the wall!

Another secret panel!

She froze. The thudding had paused.

Have they heard you?

Taylor flew up the last short flight to the landing and grasped the ring with no thought as to what or who she might find behind the panel, it was somehow imperative not to be caught in the stairwell. Only as the wall gave to her tug did she remember the screech of the panel in Julius's room.

Quietly, she pleaded.

Obediently it swung open without a sound. Taylor pushed through into a darkened room the minute there was space enough to fit, tugging at the edges of the door to reverse its motion. Slowly — it seemed like eons to Taylor — the door responded and glided shut, settling silently into place.

Taylor turned from the wall to meet the surprised eyes of the man on the bed.

CHAPTER 29

"Laszlo!" Taylor gasped in a heavy whisper.

Suddenly she remembered him completely. Tall, dark, a hard muscled body, with eyes that seemed to drill to one's core. And not the man she saw in the car at all. He was propped up with pillows, wearing an elegant if wrinkled pair of red silk pajamas and was bound with duct tape, wrists and ankles, a piece of tape over his mouth. Laszlo moved his eyes repeatedly left to right. "Someone in the next room?" she asked softly and he nodded.

Then we'd better leave the way I came.

What about Whiny and Grumpy?

You'll have Laszlo.

A barefoot man in pajamas who's been taped up for a week, great.

Taylor was searching in her tote with one hand, looking for her Swiss Army knife to cut the tape when out of the corner of her eye she saw the secret panel moving. The bed Laszlo lay on was like the ones in her bedroom, high off the floor with a wooden set of steps to aid in mounting. That left a lot of room under the bed and Taylor dove for it. She curled at once into a ball behind the steps so a casual inspection might miss her. The dust skirt had barely settled back in place when she saw the two pair of feet, one set of brown scuffed shoes the other stylish black suede, beside the bed, inches from her face.

"You ready for your dinner? More nice bread and water? Or how about some roast lamb and onions, lots of salad, huh? All you have to do is answer a couple of questions. Got to be tired of eating the same old thing by now." There was the sound of tape ripping off week old beard and a grunt of repressed pain.

"I think he wants to play some more," a new voice said.

"You just keep your gun on our guest while I feed him like we were told. We can't get any answers from dead men."

"We don't seem to be getting any answers from a live one either," the second man groused. "I have a whole lot of frustrations I would enjoy to take out on this Russian devil."

Bet he's the one with the scuffed shoes.

Second cousin of Whiny.

That makes four minimum.

How many more?

At least one.

Two — the man in the hall and the one, possibly more, watching TV.

So far no one seems like they're really in charge.

Devil... Laszlo does have a devilish look about him.

And the heart of an angel.

The bed creaked and Taylor surmised, since the black suede shoes were now missing, that he'd sat.

"Just like feeding a damned baby," the voice Taylor had assigned to the brown shoes spat.

"You saw what he did to Altzen, you want to give him a chance at your neck?"

"Well, you know what that means, Russian, you do not get your bathroom break until the others get back. Don't see why one middle-aged woman should take so much killing, she is even more dangerous than you. We ought to have done what I said in the first place and blown them all up."

"You fool — blowing up Swiss citizens — that's all it would take to convince the Swiss to give up our money to those pigs."

"You think you know everything."

"Quit your babbling and hurry up in there."

It was a third voice, from the hallway.

"And when you go back down to the kitchen make sure you get back up here just as soon as you finish your dinner. I don't want mine cold again tonight."

For several minutes it was quiet and Taylor was filled with curiosity. Only the fact that she could still see the brown shoes kept her still.

Good thing there's not much dust under here.

Great, just thinking about it is going to make you sneeze.

I will not sneeze.

Taylor bit at her lower lip to keep the suggestion from becoming a fact.

Sneeze and it will be all too easy for them to kill this middle-aged woman.

Want to die in bed, not under it.

The two men in the bedroom conversed in what Taylor took to be the same language Grumpy had used to cuss out Whiny, laughing derisively now and again. At one point the man in the hall spoke to them sharply, they lowered their voices even further and laughed some more.

Bet what they said wasn't very nice.

Not exactly friends.

Money and terrorism makes strange bedfellows.

It's the fellow in the bed I'm worried about.

And the one under it.

Taylor felt chilled and tired.

Wish I were warm and safe in bed.

In bed with Chris.

Right.

Hungry, too.

Warm in bed with Chris and a plate of sandwiches.

And a glass of wine.

You're never satisfied.

Stop wasting your time daydreaming and figure out what you're going to do next.

Get Laszlo loose.

Get out of here.

Up the secret stairs, down the other stairs, up the road to collect help from the vineyard and home to...

...Chris, sandwiches, and wine.

Right.

After a while there was the sound of tape being ripped from a roll. "Hope you enjoyed your feast," the speaker chuckled at his joke.

The black shoes reappeared and then both sets of feet turned away. "Back in an hour," one called out.

Taylor dared to lift the edge of the dust ruffle a scant half-inch, just in time to see the secret panel come full closed.

Must be the most direct route back to the kitchen?!

Above her Laszlo bounced his feet on the bed. Taylor took it to mean the coast was clear and stuck her head out carefully. She couldn't see the door from where she was.

Then anyone outside the door can't see me.

You hope.

She lay out flat to shimmy from under the bed, dragging her tote carefully after her to keep any of the contents from rattling, wondering all the while why it hadn't hurt so much when she'd gone under. Her back hurt, her hips, her shoulders, and her neck was stiff. When Taylor began to rise, her knees threatened to buckle and her head throbbed.

You were still too long.

I want my bed.

I want Chris.

I want Advil.

That she had. But when she stuck her hand in her tote she was after the knife.

First things first.

She opened the tiny scissors, knowing from past experience that they would work best on the duct tape.

Laszlo held out his wrists and Taylor made quick work of them. She reached for the tape on his mouth but he shook his head, so she cut his ankles free. Laszlo slung his feet off the bed ignoring the tape still sticking to his pajamas. He stood, wobbled, clenched his fists, and then nodded toward the secret panel.

Taylor took it as her signal to open the way. She took a step toward the wall. Laszlo went the other way toward the open door. Alarmed Taylor started after him only to be warned back by his upraised hand. He held up one finger then pointed at her.

Stay here you'll be right back?!!!

Are you sure that's what he means?

Laszlo sidled up to the door, and stepped quickly around into the hall. There was a gasp, a soft popping sound, and Laszlo was back, pulling the tape from his mouth.

"Ouchhh! Damn, that hurts."

"What about...?" Taylor hissed pointing to the hall.

"No matter if they let his dinner get cold tonight. We'd better hurry."

"Oh." Taylor pushed at the wall and nothing happened.

Was there a latch, a secret place to press!!

Why didn't you watch when the others left.

Panicked she pushed again a bit to the right and was rewarded with instant movement. Taylor went first and started up per her plan. Laszlo grabbed her arm, shaking his head.

"Bedrooms. Where the night shift may or may not be asleep and there're two guards in the tower at all times, watching the access to the chateau, front and back. How'd you get here?"

"The tunnel, there's a tunnel between the chateaux."

"I know," Laszlo said in grim hushed tones.

He went several steps up, pulled a remaining chunk of tape from his pajama's leg and tossed it onto the flight above. "That's the way I came, too. Not voluntarily. And that's the way we need to get back."

He'd returned and started down.

"There's no other way we can leave this place and not be seen. We'd be dead before we got to the road. I've kept

193

a little secret or two from my new friends. One being I speak many languages beyond English and my native tongue. There are, it would appear, as many as two-dozen of them here at any given time and they are certain they are ready for any approach from outside. We have no reason to doubt them."

"But…" Taylor said and then realized she had no good argument. "Then we better hurry and get as far as the chapel before they come back to relieve the man in the hall for his dinner." She'd matched her actions with her words and was moving swiftly down the stairs after him.

"Chapel?" Laszlo whispered when she'd caught up.

"You'll see. Though I'd bet they'll be searching the place top to bottom the minute they find you missing."

"I'm sure you're right."

Laszlo slowed at the first floor landing, a wary eye to the door and then hurried on.

"The kitchen is in the basement. We should have some lead time if we can get past it without calling attention to ourselves."

"There are two men in the tunnel - at the other chateau - or were when I came up. If the lights are on…" Taylor hushed as they came to the basement landing, the door was closed, they continued their downward course.

"That was locked when I came up."

"It sticks. I heard them complaining."

Aren't you glad you didn't rattle that door on your way up!

It's too light below.

The widening out of the stairwell made it all too clear that the lights were on. And, Taylor noted, Laszlo was leaning heavily on the banister and not moving near as fast as he had when they started down the stairs.

"That way," Taylor said, pointing toward the chapel as they came around the final turn of the steps. "Through the door."

CHAPTER 30

Taylor stole a quick glance down the tunnel as she came off the last step and saw nothing but the lighted maw of the long tube that led to safety.

Safety, once you get past Whiny and Grumpy and find a way to get back through the looking glass at the other end.

Idiot, you left the door to the tunnel open.

They'll think Whiny and Grumpy left it open.

Until they get told different.

They'll think Laszlo left that way and not look in the chapel.

They'll go tromping down the tunnel and you'll really be cut off.

She followed Laszlo into the chapel and gently closed the door, leaning against it in the dark, her heart beating a mile a minute. Beside her she could hear that Laszlo was also breathing in gasps.

"You OK?" she whispered, searching again for her penlight.

Found, she switched it on and flashed it around the room so Laszlo could see where they were.

"Let's go sit down."

"I'm fine," he protested moving with her to one of the carved pews anyway. "Better than before you arrived. How about you?"

Taylor pointed the light into her tote and located the little metal pillbox.

"I need a pill."

"Oh?" he sounded alarmed.

"Advil. I'm kind of achy... it's a long story. Want one?"

"Two," he said, holding out his hand.

They downed their Advil sans water and Taylor told him about falling through the wall, the trip through the tunnel and Whiny and Grumpy.

"But why didn't Julius help you?"

"Julius? Julius is a cat. Marta's attic cat. A fact obviously unknown by my whiny acquaintance."

"I see," Laszlo said, chuckling. "Taylor," he said more seriously, "We have to get out of here. Every moment wasted is one closer to them finding out I'm not where they left me. I suspect they are going to be grossly unhappy about my disposing of the fellow in the hall. He's somebody's brother from what I gathered. It might be easier to face down the two in the tunnel than take on the whole house full."

"A small understatement. But there's only the one bend and then it's stick straight with no place to hide, only the three shallow alcoves, for a good three-quarters of a mile. Remember, they have guns."

"Can we turn the lights off?"

"As a matter of fact, we can," Taylor told him. "But I have no idea if there's another switch at the other end or someplace along the tunnel."

"We're going to have to take our chances. Ready?"

Taylor wasn't at all sure she was ready but she stood up anyhow, her back and legs protesting.

"We get back in time for dinner you have to promise to talk Lars out of taking us for fried cheese."

"I like fried cheese."

Back at the door Taylor switched off the penlight. "The switches for the tunnel lights are just inside the entrance to the passage, on the left."

He opened the door a crack and listened. They skirted behind the staircase and then with a quick check of the stairs hurried to the tunnel's mouth where Taylor flipped off the lights.

"Hang onto your little light, but keep it off," Laszlo said, grasping the wires that exited the switch box and ripping them free, he tucked the loose ends behind the metal box to hide his deed. "Let's keep the odds down."

As they passed through the door he closed it, putting them in total darkness. "I want to be a total surprise to anyone we should happen to meet. No talking now," he whispered softly.

Taylor trailed her right hand along the wall eager to find the first alcove. She could feel the upward tilt of the floor, it seemed to go on forever. When at last she encountered the edge of the recess and knew they had come a quarter of the way she felt a lift of spirits quickly followed by a chilling fear. They had cleared the tilt and bend in the tunnel, it was a straight shot now to the chateau and Chris – a straight shot also, for the sound of a disgruntled conversation to reach their ears.

"Some fucking funny joke."

"Maybe it's a power failure."

"It's Hassam's idea of sport."

"Slow down, step on your own feet."

"Well hurry up then so I don't keep running into you."

"It's black as the devil's belly, I don't want to trip."

"Over what you fool? There is nothing in this tunnel to trip over. Now move it."

The "fool" responded with what Taylor was sure was a derogatory description of the other man's heritage in the increasingly familiar language. His companion replied in kind. She tried to judge the distance between them but could be sure of only one thing – it was closing.

Taylor wanted to suggest going back to the alcove, or hurrying on to the next, in the hopes they could simply huddle on the bench and be passed by in the dark, but she dare not speak. Her left hand now trailed the wall, seeking the next recess. The two ahead in the dark continued to squabble, the invectives flying back and forth with great vehemence. Taylor wondered if at any minute the two men might come to blows, and still she and Laszlo hurried toward them.

Like trains, racing to meet head on.

Is Laszlo thinking straight?

Too late to question.

He's tired.

A week of bread and water and no exercise.

How fit can he be?

Looks like you're going to find out.

Fried cheese wouldn't be that bad.

The men's voices were nearly upon them — Taylor could all but feel their breath on her face. Just as her hand found the second alcove a strong arm scooped her sideways against the bench.

What! She bit back the cry.

Are we going to hide?

Laszlo's read your mind.

The approaching men were louder by the second. Taylor slid back into a corner of the bench and pulled her feet up.

Maybe this isn't such a good idea after all.

Exactly what would you do instead?

Too late now.

Taylor could hear their footfall on the stone floor feet, if not inches, away. Suddenly one fell silent mid-tirade.

"What?" the other queried crossly. "Answer me! Hey?" he lapsed briefly into his native tongue and then the dark tunnel went quiet, followed in quick order by a resounding crack.

Head against stone!

Whose head?

There was only the sound of heavy breathing.

Who?

Taylor's heart was beating so hard, so fast, and loud that she felt sure the panting man would know he was not alone. She was still clutching the penlight, her fingers ached she held it so tightly.

Turn it on.

Shine it in his eyes and run.

"Turn on the light, I want to find their guns."

It was Laszlo. Instantly the small beam was on, still aimed at the panting, it struck him full in the face and she could see he was pale and in pain.

"On the floor," he directed, but not before Taylor saw the dark stain spreading on his left shoulder. "We may need the guns. There's a knife, too."

Taylor stood and flashed the light across the floor illuminating the two bodies. One slumped neatly against the wall the other crumpled in a heap at Laszlo's feet. Breathing in gasps he searched the men, coming away in the end with three guns and two knives.

"Sit a minute," Taylor suggested.

"Best not. I'm not sure I have the energy to take on the rest of them just yet, even with this arsenal, and it occurs to me that if they have taken the time to light this tunnel they may also have booby-trapped it. Terrorists are big on blowing things up. It might be a very good idea to get out of here with some speed. Once they know I've gotten away they may want to cover their tracks."

"On that cheery thought..." Taylor said and pointed the light in the appropriate direction.

"One thing first. Help me," he said.

Taylor lay the light on the bench and they dragged, then stuffed, the two men under it.

"Now their comrades will have to come this far before they know for sure that we left this way." He tucked an arm that had flopped out across the floor back out of sight with obvious effort and gave Taylor a smile.

"Let's go, Chris will undoubtedly have kept Lars from his dinner just to look for you."

"Your shoulder..."

"When we are out of here," Laszlo cut her off, striding forward with determination.

199

He did not pause when they passed the last of the alcoves and Taylor could do nothing but follow behind, keeping the light, which seemed to be growing dimmer, pointed just ahead of the wounded man.

Batteries are beginning to go.

Lucky they lasted this long.

Going to be fun climbing those ladders in the dark!

Maybe Laszlo can unstick the top ladder.

If he lasts that long.

Dying batteries.

Dying man.

Adds up to a dying Taylor.

Chris is looking for you.

So are the terrorists by now.

Oh goody, a contest.

"Not far now," Taylor said, seeing the stone steps and broken door that signaled the end of the tunnel. "It's not quite as nice as the other end but the occupants are friendlier."

"You have got to be kidding," Laszlo said when they'd reached the wooden platform and the first of the aluminum ladders.

"Isn't this the way they took you?" Taylor asked.

"I was knocked out in the bedroom and didn't come to until we were halfway through the tunnel. I killed one before they hit me over the head again. Must have been a chore, getting me down the ladder. Up we go."

"Wait, let me wrap this around your shoulder, you're losing a lot of blood."

"You were planning on a sleep over?"

He grunted but held still while she knotted the peach silk pajama bottoms in place.

Laszlo climbed slowly with only one hand to steady himself, his left arm hanging limp at his side.

"Walter Altzen," Taylor said.

"What about him?"

"That's who you killed in the tunnel."

"Couldn't have happened to a nicer fellow."

Laszlo had reached the basement platform and gallantly offered Taylor his good hand to steady her way off the ladder's top.

"Up again?"

"Have to. No door here, just four very solid walls. Actually," she said as they again climbed, "Our best bet is at the top. I couldn't find a way out on the first floor either and the handle of the panel into your bedroom is broken."

The beam of the little flashlight was fading fast, illuminating a bare three or four-feet ahead and that very dimly.

Taylor had the feeling it was not only the beam that was fading. Laszlo climbed slower, even more deliberately than at first. When they reached the platform on the second floor of the chateau he stopped to lean against the ladder and rest.

"I guess it's too late to thank them," Taylor said.

"I don't understand," Laszlo replied.

"The ladder. When I saw it last it was stuck, half off the landing. Our pals from the tunnel must have pulled it loose and set it straight so they could go looking for me. For Julius and I."

As she spoke the penlight went out completely.

"Drat. Guess we go the last bit in the dark."

Though Laszlo was only two feet away Taylor could not see him. Disorientation mixed with fear flashed through her. Taylor felt his hand bump into her shoulder and hold it firmly just long enough for Taylor to settle her panic and remember where they'd been standing and where the ladder should be.

"Here we go," he said.

The only way Taylor could tell he was climbing was to fumble forward until her foot knocked into the ladder.

Go ahead, knock it sideways again.

201

"You okay?" she asked quickly, feeling the ladder and running her hands up until she encountered Laszlo's legs just above her head.

"I will be when we're through playing blind man's bluff."

Taylor was three steps up the ladder behind him when the lights came on below them casting an eerie glow up through the series of ladders and landings. "Well, that's helpful."

"I should have demolished the switch box, they've reconnected it. I suggest we make sure we aren't still on the ladder when they get here," Laszlo said, climbing faster. "If they are put out now they are going to be even more so when they get to the middle of the tunnel."

He'd reached the top, the ring hung very handily in front of him and he gave it a tug. "Watch your head," he said as, with its usual screech, the door swung inward.

CHAPTER 31

"Should have known I'd find you two together."

The bright beam of Lars big flashlight hit Taylor in the face but it was Chris's voice behind it.

"How the hell did you get in the wall?"

"It wasn't easy," Taylor told him. "Now get us out of here before half your list of money laundering bad guys and their friends come pouring out with us."

Chris had already grasped Laszlo by his good arm and aided him across the space between the top of the ladder and the edge of the floor. He reached down and lifted Taylor up and through the opening. By the time he'd set her on her feet the wall was swinging closed.

"You OK?"

"I am, mostly. Laszlo's not, he needs a doctor."

"First, we need to arrange a raid on the chateau up the road, and as quickly as possible," Laszlo said and started for the door. "Then some food, and then the doctor."

"May I suggest we also find a way to see that they can't come through the secret panels here," Taylor added breaking from Chris's arms to hurry after Laszlo.

"We've got men here and ready with backup on the way, so the raid's no problem," Chris thrust the flashlight into Taylor's hand. "You two take your time, I'll get the show on the road," he called over his shoulder taking long strides toward the stairs that led to Marta's laundry room.

"There are two in the tower watching the road," Laszlo called after him. "Undoubtedly well armed."

Chris acknowledged the info with a raise of a fist and kept going.

When Taylor and Laszlo reached the laundry room they were met by two heavily armed men in black who rattled away excitedly in both French and Italian. "Are they on our side?"

"Yes," Laszlo told her. "They want to know where the secret panels are."

"I wondered how we were going to block doors that opened out. I'll show one the third floor panel if you'll tell him to come with me. The other one is on this floor, the wall beside your bed, the handle's broken but..."

Laszlo gave instructions in Italian and one of the black clad men raised his automatic weapon in salute and nodded for her to lead the way. Taylor knew she was operating on pure adrenaline and even that was running short. Her feet were leaden as she climbed back up the steps to the third floor.

You're safe now, quit stressing.

Not safe until they're all caught.

Or dead.

Would be nice if they'd leave at least one alive long enough to tell us exactly what it is has them so anxious to see you dead.

Nice would be a hot shower, clean clothes, and dinner.

"There," Taylor flashed the beam across the left wall of Julius' room. "The door is there, esta," she said in Spanish knowing the word was similar in Italian.

She motioned with her arm to show how the door swung in. The man aimed his own bright beam at the wall and waved her out. Taylor fled gladly back to Marta's apartment.

Laszlo was not in his room. The man set to guard the secret panel motioned her away from the door from his position on the far side of the bed.

A death trap for anyone coming through either of those secret panels.

Bet these are the men from the back garden.

Chris and Lars will be going into the other chateau with the men from the house in the vineyard.

About the two armed men on the third floor — dead before we got to the road, Laszlo said!

Chris has done this before.

He's supposed to be writing textbooks so other people can do it.

Never seems to work out that way.

I think he enjoys it.

She found Laszlo in the great room sitting on the bench at the dining table, the wide-eyed Gretchen dabbing at his shoulder with a damp cloth. He was pale but he managed a small smile.

"Lars said it was better she waited until the excitement was over," Adie said from the kitchen. "There will be soup soon."

"Marta..." Taylor said...

"I called Elsbeth's and Marta will stay there until I call again. I think they are put out to miss being in the center of things," Adie said smugly.

"I wouldn't have minded missing some of it," Taylor said. "I feel like we are about to be under siege."

"There is about to be a siege," Laszlo agreed. "At the other chateau. We are only on the lookout for escaping rats."

Taylor noted the guns and knives he'd collected in the tunnel laid out neatly on the table before him. Gretchen said something softly to Laszlo in French and then poured a clear liquid from a brown bottle onto a bit of gauze and placed it over the nasty gash below his left shoulder. Taylor saw his even white teeth grit together. At that moment the siege well and truly broke out up the road. Gunfire, lots of it. Sirens joined the frightening serenade and flashing blue and red lights shone through the windows as vehicles flew along the road.

"Eat," Adie ordered, setting a tray with two bowls of steaming vegetable soup on the table. "Soup is good for shock. Then you will explain this," she waved a hand in the direction of all the noise, "to me, please. Lars said only that you had been taken by some very bad men."

She returned to the kitchen for the bread and cheese.

The battle sounded closer than the intervening mile and the amount of gunfire had picked up after the sirens stopped. Taylor sipped at the soup without really tasting it, her inner council revving up for a debate on the wisdom of checking the activity on the second and third floor.

They'd have to come through the secret panels one at a time and...

More sirens and then bright lights as one or more vehicles pulled noisily into the chateau's drive. There was at once a pounding at the door. Adie got there first. "You must evacuate," the man said without ceremony when she opened it.

"I am Swiss. I do not leave my home," Adie said in a voice that brooked no argument. She added some quick words of Italian that brought a sharp protest from Laszlo's nurse.

"We will be staying as well," Taylor said, precluding Laszlo sending her off.

She was sure he would not go himself.

"The men upstairs might need some reinforcement, I'll show you the way. Oh, and we could use a doctor or a paramedic if there is one."

Laszlo sent her a dark glare but said nothing. In short order Taylor was leading six men in modern armor across the balcony to Marta's apartment and Gretchen was in a police car on her way home.

Her hand was on the apartment door when Taylor realized the sounds of gunfire were not all coming from across the zucchini fields. "Left across the living room, last room on the left this floor," she said standing out of the way. "And last door on the right and up the stairs," she called after them.

Taylor leaned back against the stone wall shaking as the small war escalated.

You wanted to stay — why?

Chris.

And why are you standing here?

"Good question," Taylor turned toward the stairs.

The sky lit up and a chain of horrific concussions echoed off the nearby mountains.

"Chris," Taylor screamed and fled across the balcony and down the steps.

Adie and Laszlo, barefooted and bare chested, the throw from the couch wrapped around him, were already headed down the drive behind the running police officer who halted them all in the road. The sky was orange and great columns of flame and smoke rose up behind the black outline of the trees. Then a cascade of muted explosions tossed dirt and plants skyward, raining black blobs against the orange, in a line coming across the fields toward them.

"It is like a war," the policeman gasped.

"The war did not come so close," Adie said, gripping at Taylor's arm though it was defiance not fear in her voice.

Black smoke roiled toward them and over it all more sirens could be heard coming from town. There was a final tremendous explosion that lit the night and echoed like thunder and then there was only sirens and smoke. Even the gunfire in the chateau behind them had ceased.

Laszlo had his good arm around her shoulders and Adie still clung to her other side.

Holding you back.

Holding you up.

Holding them up.

"Chris," Taylor said, not a cry but a prayer.

Ambulances arrived and a crowd grew behind the police blockade at the corner that included amazed and curious locals as well as big media vans. Marta and Elsbeth would not be stopped and pushed through to join Adie, and to stare in wonder as stretchers came from the chateau behind them, most with bodies in bags, three with injured.

"We'll want to talk to them," Laszlo reminded the official beside him, never taking his eyes from the smoky glow a mile up the road. "Later."

Only Adie's steel grip and the sagging weight of Laszlo kept Taylor from running forward. She stared into the acrid haze that with the fire behind it now turned the black night a sickly orange. More fire trucks disappeared into the miasma, more armored and camouflaged beings — it was impossible to tell male, female or extraterrestrial — arrived and some swarmed up the drive and into the chateau, the rest followed the fire trucks. Eventually an ambulance was signaled forward as well. Taylor's chest was tightening, her breathing becoming a deliberate effort. She knew she was going to need a pill and she could not remember where she'd left her tote.

You gave Laszlo Advil in the chapel.

You wrapped your pajamas around his knife wound at the bottom of the stair shaft.

In the great room, you left it there when you took the new men up to Marta's apartment.

How can a stone building burn so?

She couldn't make herself go in, not even for the pills. Taylor worked to control her breathing and her stress, biting the inside of her cheek to keep focus. Minutes that felt like hours passed. An errant breeze fanned the flames causing them to leap higher, dispersing the smoke across the river. The lights on the ambulance were clearly visible and her heart leapt when it appeared to be moving back toward them, then it made the turn at that far away corner and, siren blaring, sped off.

"Who?" Laszlo demanded of the man beside him who Taylor noticed only now was wearing a headset and exchanging information in soft Italian.

"Helmutter, one of the swat team — a minor wound — and one of the Interpol men — overcome by smoke. The rest are still watching for any survivors and keeping back the curious from that end.

Taylor was sorry for Helmutter and the Interpol man but she was also relieved. Her lightheadedness eased and her breathing as well.

Edward arrived and for once said not a word to Elsbeth. He did take his jacket off and wrap it around Adie's shoulders.

"Such a beautiful restoration," he observed sadly.

The army in camouflage that had swarmed into the chateau swarmed out again.

"You may go back in. It is smoky but safe. The tunnel is collapsed, it goes a quarter mile now, no more," the officer reported.

"Did they check the tombs," Taylor asked. "You could hide a dozen places..."

"They have checked every inch, there is no one who has not been dead a very long time."

You forgot about Petra!

Not the time to mention her now.

Edward drew Adie away from her side and back up the driveway with Elsbeth and Marta trailing behind talking excitedly. Laszlo, like Taylor, seemed disinclined to move though his weight sagged more heavily on her.

At last men began to drift back, black figures against the glow at first, then sooty ghosts dissolving out of the night, recognizable features coming clear only as they closed the last few yards between them.

Taylor flung herself at one such sooty ghost, "Darling, are you OK?"

"I'm fine, Lars is a little singed," Chris replied hugging her fiercely. "I could drink a river."

Lars, great chunks of his hair and beard charred or missing, was sooty, head to foot.

"This, boys and girls, is what Saint Nicholas looks like when he gets stuck in a chimney," Laszlo said as his friend greeted him with a bear hug.

"You could both use a shower and some clean clothes," Taylor said, continuing to cling to Chris. "Did they blow up their chateau or did you?"

"A bit of both I think. You aren't exactly a fashion poster yourself. Hey!" Chris let loose of her to help Lars with a crumbling Laszlo.

"Hungry," Laszlo mumbled.

He refused the ambulance insisting all he really needed was to be allowed to finish his soup.

"Either you let the doctor put a couple of stitches in that wound or I will," Adie threatened when they'd deposited him on the sofa. "I'll call him. Marta can heat the soup."

"Not bleeding anymore," Laszlo grumbled but argued no further, accepting gratefully the glass of red wine Edward poured for him.

"Elsbeth can heat the soup," Marta said. "I want to see what kind of a mess has been made of my apartment."

"Heat lots of soup, please," Lars said. I will go take a shower."

He was examining himself in the mirror over the sideboard.

"Perhaps I should go on a diet. I move too slow and am too big of a target."

"No holes in you," Chris told him. "I'd say you moved fast enough."

"But look at my poor beard," Lars sighed.

CHAPTER 32

Laszlo was left to Adie and Elsbeth's ministrations. Taylor'd caught sight of herself in the mirror and found she looked almost as dirty and disheveled as Chris and Lars.

"Clean clothes and showers all round," she declared picking up her tote and heading for the door.

"Now there's an offer I can't refuse," Chris said, following her. "Not real interested in letting you out of my sight right now either," he said as they climbed the stairs. "And, I'm dying to hear how you and Laszlo managed to find each other."

"I found him."

Taylor and Chris arrived back in the great room in time to watch the doctor finish the last of three stitches in Laszlo's shoulder and put a bandage – a big waterproof Band-Aid really – over them.

"And a tetanus shot, I think," the doctor said, dipping into his bag and coming out with a ready filled syringe. "You are looking well, Mrs. Robbins. You have remembered, yes?"

Taylor had taken a pill, had a hot shower – with Chris to scrub her back – and was feeling better mentally and physically than she had in days.

"I've remembered nearly everything. There are a few things – the last minutes before I went in the ditch, the accident itself – that I can't recall. Not totally anyhow."

"It will come, perhaps, but sometimes, never." he said, administering the shot. "Now, I must get back to my family and tell them it was not this chateau that blew up. You will get lots of rest and eat lots of Adie and Marta's good food and get well," the doctor instructed Laszlo, exiting as Lars returned.

"Oh, my," Taylor exclaimed. He'd all but shaved his head bald, and his white beard, nearly as short and shaped to a point at the chin, it made him look very martial.

"There was no other way," Lars said. "It was burned to the scalp in some places. Marta helped me. I feel as if my head has shrunk and is too small for my body."

He cut a thick slab of bread.

"After we eat we must go identify the dead and talk to the survivors," he turned to Laszlo, "You will be up to the task?"

"Another bowl of soup and some more of that cold chicken and I'm all yours," Laszlo said. "But first I, too, need to clean up."

He rose, wobbled but held up a hand to stave off help. "I shall manage."

"Your room is chaos," Marta warned him. "But at least no one will be coming through the wall."

Taylor could see Laszlo's color was returning but there were dark shadows under his eyes.

"Couldn't the identifying bit wait until tomorrow?"

"No," he said before either Chris or Lars could speak. "We must know as soon as possible what rats are dead and which ones are still out there. I am the only one who saw the men in the house, heard them speak."

He walked none too steadily toward the door.

"Drat, I forgot my pipe," Lars said. "I'll come up with you. Taylor, I want to hear your adventure, eat only, until I get back please."

When Lars returned, Taylor had inhaled her bowl of soup and was savoring bread and cheese accompanied by a second glass of wine.

"Now," Lars said, settling comfortably in his chair. "Tell us how you found your way into the tunnel."

"When I was a boy I looked everywhere and you find it with no help," Edward said, refilling his own glass and topping up any of the others that needed it.

"Quiet, Edward and let her tell," Adie said. "Elsbeth be sure the soup stays warm."

"Quiet, yourself," Edward snapped.

By the time Taylor'd finished explaining about the dust on Julius's floor and falling through the wall, the ladders and rotted stairs and begun on the mausoleum, Laszlo had returned. Clean shaven, in black slacks and cream silky sweater he looked a million miles removed from the world he'd lived in for the last week.

"Have you told them about hiding under the bed yet?" he asked.

"Not yet. I was about to tell them about Petra."

"Who's Petra?" Chris asked. "What bed?"

But he was drowned out by the exclamations of Edward and his sisters.

"Petra disappeared more than a half century ago," Lars told Chris.

"And I found her," Taylor said. "She must have fallen through the wall just like I did. Adie, you said she used to go up there to daydream. I'll bet she used to sit on the floor and lean against the wall — that day the wood or metal hasp, whatever was used to keep it shut, gave way and she fell. I'm not sure how she found the tomb with the cherubs carved on it but she was there, behind a bench. It was the blue ribbons, that's how I knew it was her."

"But we must get her out, at once," Adie said, standing as if she meant to do it that minute.

"Adie," Edward said, "It has been a very long time. Petra, and God, will forgive us for waiting one more day. The doctor must come. It is a legal thing," he explained. "The doctor and the police, to file the proper report so we can bury her. To think, she was always here."

There were tears streaming down his face, Adie was pale, her hands knotted in her apron, Elsbeth and Marta had turned their heads away. It was Marta who sniffed

213

loudly and raised her head, "So, then you went the other way, into the tunnel?"

"...and the door came open and there was Chris shining a light right in our eyes," Taylor concluded her saga. "Come to think of it, what made you think of looking for me up there?"

"Chalk another one up for Julius. We'd looked everywhere, searched the chateau top to bottom — both sets of agents swore you never left the grounds. Lars and the others started searching the gardens and the fields, I went up for another flashlight — I was going to check the garden shed. The cat had only followed us around when we searched the third floor, guess he expected us to find you without his help. Now he was howling, sitting right over our bedroom. I figured if he'd been howling earlier, you'd have gone to see why. When I got up to where he was sitting Julius scooted off to what you call his room, and howled some more. Then I noticed just what you did. Not enough dust, and footprints when you held the light just right, footprints right up to the wall. I was pondering the whole idea when, there you were.

"Remind me to slip Julius some sardines," Taylor laughed. "It is a shame the beautiful mosaics in the tunnel have been destroyed, and the chapel. A fire might have left the walls, but those explosions..."

"They had a considerable store of munitions and explosives," Lars said. "I'm not sure all of it was defensive, though we may never know what plans they had."

"Or who triggered the explosions," Chris added. "Certainly, the tunnel was rigged to blow on purpose."

"But how did they know we'd be here?" Taylor asked. "They had to have been at this for more than a year."

"A very good question, darling," Chris said, standing. "And since Lars and Laszlo have finished off the soup, not to mention the bread and cheese, I think it's time we had a talk with the survivors and see if we can get some answers."

Edward and his sisters seemed more shocked by the finding of Petra than their close encounter with terrorists of a tunnel kind. They'd known that Lars' frequent business in Switzerland was confidential, and from things said, perhaps they had suspected it was also dangerous.

They never suspected it was quite so dangerous to them personally.

I'm the one the terrorists were after.

You... and Chris and Lars... and Laszlo.

They'd have killed anyone who got in the way, including Adie and Marta.

Nothing explains how they knew we'd be here?

A mole of some kind.

The idea of a mole and the tunnel tickled her and she giggled.

"Taylor?" Chris asked eyeing her with concern.

"Just a little tired," Taylor covered.

Edward fell back into his mold and insisted on escorting Elsbeth home.

"I will come in the morning and we will have the doctor and the police go with us to take care of Petra. And I will see to it the secret doors are sealed."

Taylor saw Adie open her mouth and then snap it shut and she suspected there would be further conversation on the subject out of company's hearing. After Edward and Elsbeth left, Adie and Marta went to straighten what they could of Marta's apartment.

"Can I come too?" Taylor asked, seeing the men preparing to leave.

"Not a good place for you to be, darling, and we may be very late." Chris said. "You need some rest."

"Laszlo needs some rest, too," she said unwilling to let the subject go.

"I just spent a week in bed, if anything, I am over rested," the Russian protested.

"Interpol is still watching the chateau," Lars said. "Now that the tunnel is gone, you can sleep without worry."

"I'm more curious than afraid, I want to know why me. But is a guard really necessary?" Taylor asked. "Is what's at stake so much they'll continue?"

"Yes," Lars answered. "Many billions with what we have learned. Until we are sure they were all killed or captured we must keep a watch."

"Billions, WOW! Well then, Laszlo," Taylor said, "maybe you know what I saw or did that had them more determined to kill me than Lars or Chris? Did any of them ever talk about it?"

"I heard mention of the American woman on the bicycle..."

"That was me," Taylor nodded her head in encouragement.

"The fellow talking was putting down someone named Radzic for not doing a good job of killing you in the first place. They thought it was very funny."

"What did I ever do to Radzic?"

"That," Laszlo said with a raised eyebrow, "They never said."

"Which is why," Chris said, dropping a kiss on the top of her head, "we need to know more before we assume that we, and you in particular, are no longer in danger from this source at least."

Taylor took Advil to combat the stiffness and aches creeping into her body and went to bed, couldn't sleep, tried to read and, of course, fell asleep at once. She dreamed fitfully, coming full awake at what she was sure was the screeching sound of the panel in Julius's room closing.

You were asleep.

Dreaming.

I heard the secret panel, a stubborn voice insisted.

All in your head.

Silent as a tomb now.

Punny, the critic sneered.

She wanted to believe, was too tired not to believe. Taylor put her book on the nightstand, turned off the light and slid deeper under the downy coverlet.

"Chris will be home soon," she reminded herself — warning the air about her.

She slept to dream of fleeing through endless tunnels that were sometimes dark, sometimes bright as day and at other times exploding, sending her running from falling stone, fire and smoke. Then Chris was home, she felt his warm body fold around her, felt the welcome weight of his arm across her and she slept again.

CHAPTER 33

Breakfast was barely over when Edward arrived. On his heels were the doctor looking slightly unsettled and a plainclothes policeman who dwarfed Lars' six-foot plus frame in both height and girth. "I am in charge of what you call Cold Cases," he said with slight German overtones. "Where is this missing child?"

"In the basement," Edward explained.

The doctor and the policeman looked distressed.

"The sub-basement really," Taylor corrected. "And, we'll have to go up to get down. I'll have to show you."

"It is not necessary..." Edward began.

"We are all going," Adie said firmly. "We must see for ourselves."

Edward said no more, even when Elsbeth joined them as they started up the stairs. Taylor led the solemn parade across the balcony and through Marta's apartment.

"She fell from the next floor up," Taylor told the policeman, "but it will be easier for us to go down through here." Laszlo's bedroom looked as spotlessly clean as the first time Marta had shown it to her. Or it did until one noticed the dark spots on the floor next to the wall that hid the panel, the splatter of chinks in stone and wood where bullets had made their mark, and the empty frame that once held a mirror.

"You just push," Taylor gave the wall a shove and it pivoted away from her. "We should block it open, I'm not sure how they opened it from the inside last night."

"I will stay here and see it stays open," Laszlo said. "I think I have had enough of ladders."

The landing was small, they proceeded slowly, climbing one at a time down to the next levels with Lars, bringing up (down) the rear.

On the first floor the policeman and Chris both stopped to peer through the hole into Piet's closet.

"This wall is newer," Edward proclaimed at the basement level. "No more than a couple hundred years old, see the difference in the mortar."

The doctor had some trouble on the ladders due to the medical bag he carried.

What does he expect to find?

Petra is beyond tetanus shots and Band-Aids.

They collected, like a tour group in a cavern at the bottom, their flashlights dancing across the frescos and the casket filled niches.

"That way is the tunnel," Taylor told them pointing a much larger light than she'd had the day before toward the opening. The lights they carried did not reach as far as the collapse, but the floor was littered with small bits of stone and thick dust. "And the burial chambers, where Petra is, are over here.

"The doctor had taken to murmuring "Oh, my." at every new sight or bit of information. Everyone else remained silent. Taylor moved toward the opening between the tombs, almost reluctant to be the instigator of so much traffic in a place that had been unvisited in so long. This time she noted there were holders for candles set into the stone, and names carved on the ends of the caskets.

"She's behind the bench, at the end," Taylor said. "I saw the blue ribbon.... I... Maybe, Adie, you and Marta and Elsbeth shouldn't look."

"I am not expecting to see her as we knew her," Adie stated flatly.

She pushed to the front followed by Marta, Elsbeth, and Edward. Their flashlights lit the end of the passage and the ornate tomb, casting out all shadow. The blue ribbons leapt from the gray on gray of the stone and marble.

Adie stepped up to the bench, "Mamma and Papa will be glad to see you," she said. "Though, perhaps, they know already where you have been hiding." She cleared her throat, "What must be done to get her out of here and buried properly?"

"It must be determined how she died if the doctor cannot immediately tell us," said the policeman. "If it can be determined it was an accident, then he signs a death certificate to that effect and I close the case, that is all that will be needed."

"How did the child find her way here?" Lars asked what Taylor had been pondering.

"These bones have been disturbed," the doctor said.

"Animals?" Edward asked quickly.

"Possibly, but..." He opened his bag and removed a small folding carryall that he sat on the bench and then lined with a large plastic sheet. I should know more after I have reassembled the bones."

"Foul play?" the large policeman asked.

The doctor did not answer. He was focused on removing the bones gently from where they lay.

"Oh..." Taylor said quietly reaching for Chris's hand. "I didn't think of that."

Maybe bad men, even then, knew of the secret stairs.

The stairs were rotted away — gone.

Could have happened since.

The sad but mystical tale of a child long lost then found in the company of cherubs had been replaced by thoughts of frightening violence. The quiet resting-place of the chateau's first occupants had become a crime scene. The return to the second floor was accomplished without speaking. The carryall was handed reverently up the ladders, the doctor departing with it at once. The policeman asked to be shown the place the girl might have fallen from.

"I'll take him," Chris volunteered.

"Coffee," Marta said. "We need coffee."

They sipped at their coffee in silence, each deep in their own thoughts, mourning a child, a sister, so long lost. Adie passed a plate of cookies and even Lars declined. When at last the policeman had gone, Edward departed, and Elsbeth and Marta went to sit with Adie in her apartment.

"Do you have a meeting today, after all the commotion last night?" Taylor asked Chris.

"After lunch. We need to bring the Swiss governmental representatives up to speed and to a lesser degree the bankers."

"And put a watch on a couple of accounts," Lars said. "Some cheese in the trap."

"Trap?" Taylor echoed. "Then someone did escape?" She turned to Laszlo, "Someone you saw, while they were holding you, he wasn't among the dead or wounded?"

"More someone I didn't see. I heard them talk of a man, the organizer, they called him. I recognized the men in custody, the ones in the hospital and all of those in the morgue. There should be a least one more body."

"They could find him yet," Chris said quickly. "They've just begun searching the ruins. But until we know for sure you're still under house arrest." He smiled at her to take out some of the sting. "At least this time we won't be leaving you right where he wants you."

"Goody," Taylor whined. "Have you ever noticed that every time we go on what is supposed to be, and I quote, "more of a vacation than an assignment," things get downright nasty."

"You're not having a good time?" Chris teased lightly. "Perhaps you haven't remembered yet that you are perfectly capable of getting into trouble without me."

"I'm observant," Taylor said. "What I saw this time, or didn't see, or heard, or... I don't know what else - it might not be about this missing bad guy. If I were him I'd be busy getting myself out of here with my hide intact."

"In which case, we are being over cautious," Chris said. "A side I feel just fine erring on. In the meantime, you stay here."

"The three wounded men," Taylor asked, clutching at straws, "they didn't say anything that might give me a hint?"

"Taylor, darling," Chris said, pulling her close, "It's a good thing you are such a cute little nag."

He kissed her soundly, ignoring the presence of Lars and Laszlo completely.

"Exhibitionist," Taylor huffed.

When he released her she was smiling.

CHAPTER 34

Elsbeth stayed to lunch, the talk around the table centered on speculation about the when and why of the discontinued use of the tunnel and the walling in of the basement access to the stairs.

"Before the last of the original family left," Marta opined. They would not have wanted strangers to be storing their wine and grain where their ancestors were interred."

"The stairs at the other end were very new. I think they must have originally closed up both ends," Taylor said. "The murals and the mosaics in the tunnel were beautiful. It's a shame they're lost."

"Not truly lost," Adie said, speaking for the first time during the meal. "Some bright university student will dig up the zucchini field some day, find the pieces and people will see them in a museum. Marta, we must ask the doctor to return Petra's ribbons. I want to put them in Mamma's bible."

Adie'd made polenta again, sitting, stoic, in the heat of the fireplace beating the cornmeal mush with the wooden paddle for nearly an hour before it was ready to be turned out on the ancient board. Taylor'd needed no instructions today to make the polenta and cheese "sandwich" to be sauced with a thick herbed lamb and mushroom ragout.

"I think the stairs should be rebuilt," Elsbeth said out of the blue. "Edward could do it. And electricity, so they aren't in the dark any longer. I will pay for it, it is for the chateau so it will please him."

"A fine idea, but first he will make Petra a casket," Adie said, decisively, "and we will celebrate her life. You must all be here, without you we would never have found her. Lars you will pass me the carrots, please, I believe I am hungry."

"I'll be back in a couple of hours," Chris promised. "Even if I have to leave these two behind. And tonight we'll go to the alehouse for fried cheese."

"What is it with you men and fried cheese?" Taylor sighed.

"You will love it," Lars assured her. "Come, the sooner we go the sooner we get back."

Taylor watched the black sedan until it turned the corner and then went back to the great room where the sisters were talking quietly. They were seated at the dining table, heads bent over a large photo album.

"Come see," Marta invited.

There weren't many pictures of their childhood. In one a shy, five-year-old Petra peeked from behind Edward. In another she sat cross-legged on the floor beside a toddler Elsbeth with the elder siblings lined formally behind.

"Such a pretty child," Taylor said. "You can see the sparkle in her eyes."

"An imp," Adie agreed.

The sisters shared stories of their childhood until they were all laughing, crying, and then laughing some more.

Eventually Marta went to walk Elsbeth home and do some errands. Adie went to put the precious photo album away and Taylor was at loose ends. A persistent fine mist had turned the partly cloudy sky a solid gray - too wet to be in the garden, too damp to even sit on the porch or balcony. Taylor's curiosity about the chateau up the road rankled at her.

You might see from Marta's back fire escape.
Stay out of trouble.
What harm can there be in seeing what I can see?
You can wave at the men in the back garden.
You're going to be sorry.
Ridiculous!
One quick peek — just to see if it's still burning.

Taylor hurried up the steps, ostensibly to tuck her pajama tops under her pillow, she wondered briefly what had become of the bottoms last seen wrapped around Laszlo's chest. Leaving her tote on the bed she wandered out on the balcony.

The door is probably locked.

But when she tried Marta's door it was open.

When she stepped out on the fire escape Taylor peered through the mist toward the stand of trees but could see no sign of the men she knew were there.

Staying back out of the rain.

Wondering why you aren't doing the same.

Taylor smiled and waved anyway, then leaned out to find the view less than satisfactory. Trees, both nearby and at the far end of the field next to the other road, efficiently screened the other chateau, or what was left of it, from her sight. She did think she perceived smoke still rising.

Rain.

Steam.

You're getting soaked.

Taylor waved again in the direction of the near trees and went back inside. She was three steps inside the door, headed for the living room, when a perfectly elegant man stepped out of Lars' room to confront her. Slender, medium height, dressed in black head to toe — silk shirt open at the throat, expensive trousers, expensive shoes, strong hands, dark hair, and dark eyes.

"Piet! Hello!" Taylor said startled. "I didn't know you were back."

I didn't remember you were the man in the sedan.

The man in the bank.

Supposed to be in Paris.

"How was Paris?"

A slow smile spread over his face. Far from being reassuring it sent a cold chill up her spine.

What, or rather who you saw that you shouldn't, in the flesh!!!

But I'd already been knocked into the ditch?!

No other possible answer.

Doesn't make sense!

"My dear woman you do have a facility for turning up in all the wrong places," Piet told her. "You have cost me, and my cause, dearly. It was inevitable you would remember, eventually. Now you will pay before you do any more harm."

Taylor couldn't think of a thing to say. She stood there, what she knew was a silly half smile stuck on her face, her mind racing, remembering, parts of the puzzle now falling into place.

"Getting knocked in the ditch was just an accident, a hit and run sort of thing," she said, "Wasn't it?"

"Not entirely. Radzic was not very fond of Americans, he knew you were the woman from the chateau, an American. He edged you off the road on purpose. He was also a fool. If he was going to kill you he should have done the job, not played little boy games."

There was now a formidable black gun in his hand, pointed at her.

Must have been tucked in his belt, at the back. Would have spoiled the line of his slacks to carry it in a pocket.

I told you you should stay downstairs.

Why is he still here?

How?

Must be a door on the first floor after all.

"You built a door, a different kind of door, from your studio into the secret stairwell."

"I built the studio to hide the sound of construction and it gave me an excuse to be around, to find out when your friend Lars would be visiting. I have been watching him for years. Wherever he goes, some one of the faithful is caught, funds are impounded."

"You heard the legend about the tunnel, bought the other chateau, did all this to protect your money laundering schemes?"

"Something like that. Now, I think we should continue our tete-a-tete in safer surroundings."

He motioned toward Laszlo's door with the muzzle of the gun. "After you."

"Don't you think my husband will look for me in the tunnel?" she asked, moving as slowly as she thought she could get away with.

"Undoubtedly. But we shall be in the studio. And when they are all once more busy searching I shall take my leave until they have all left permanently. Eventually it may amuse me to return and console the dear ladies for the loss of their new friend."

Sounds like he's got his plans made.

What do you do now?

Think!

Think fast!

Taylor stumbled entering Laszlo's bedroom, sending one of the neatly lined up shoes tumbling.

"Through the wall, now," he hissed.

When they were on the landing, he gave the door a shove, hurrying it shut. A bright light shining out of a narrow opening, a board's width in the wooden wall a flight below, now open, sent a pale glow up the shaft to them.

"I know you can manage to climb down unassisted. Be very sure I have no qualms about shooting you now, but it would be so messy. Much easier, for us both, if you will be obedient."

"You moved Petra, the bones of the little girl." Taylor knew she was right. "She was at the bottom of the shaft. She fell all the way, didn't she? And you moved her, put her behind the bench, near the cherubs. Why?"

"One must have respect for the dead," he said, "And she was in the way."

Again he waved the gun, motioning her to move down the ladder.

"You sent your friends up the ladders, to their death, to cover your escape."

"They died in glory, serving their god. I am a bit more practical. I preferred to live; to enjoy the life supplying the needs of such devout men affords me. Their sacrifice and yours are as nothing to me."

When Taylor reached the first floor landing she watched Piet, one hand on the ladder, sidling down so as to keep an eye, and the gun, on her. It was dark below and there was no exit now. "Are you going to leave me in the tunnel?"

He doesn't need any suggestions from you.

Keep him talking.

Have you noticed, your heart is beating double time?

Lucky him, maybe I'll just die a natural death.

Can't let him get away with it.

Be calm.

Think, come up with something.

Open up your mouth and say something!

Right, talk him to death.

"I was going to ask to see your work, but I guess you don't really sculpt, do you?"

"I should be delighted to show you my work," he pushed the muzzle of the gun into her back and shoved her through the narrow opening into the closet.

The coats had been shoved to the side and Taylor saw him push a button on a small remote, like a garage door opener. There was a quiet hum as the panel slid back in place.

"Very modern, don't you think?" he asked.

"Very," Taylor agreed. "What now?"

Do you want to know?

"We wait. When they are busy seeking you we shall take a stroll by the river. But be sure I will do it sooner, right here, if you make it necessary."

He continued to push the gun into her ribs, propelling her forward across a hall and right, into a room directly under Marta's laundry room. Thick drapes were drawn tight blocking out all light. A small lamp glowed on a desk crowded with computers and other electronic equipment. "Communications central, my work," he said, laughing at the inside joke.

He shoved her toward one of two chrome and leather chairs, which with a hard black leather bench, were the only other furniture in the room.

"You will sit."

Taylor sat.

CHAPTER 36

Serve him right if you die right here and he has to try and carry you out without being seen.

The tightness in Taylor's chest had grown past uncomfortable and was approaching frightening pain. Mental stress exercises were not stemming the tide of fear and anger that sent her blood pressure climbing and whistled up the herd of elephants to parade at an ever-quickening pace across her chest. Taylor's hands were clammy and it was with great difficulty she was able to focus on what Piet was saying and the problem at hand. The effort only added to the stress pulling her body apart.

Calm thoughts.

Deep breaths.

No time for calm thoughts – do something!

As in?!

You need a pill.

Left the tote on the bed.

Chris will see it.

Men in the garden will tell him you were in Marta's apartment.

Tattletales.

You'd better hope so.

But he won't know I'm here.

He'll take apart the place stone by stone.

Take too long.

Breathe!

"...so you see I've been listening, heard every word said next door. It took weeks of work to get the wire through the wall. The remotes I tried at first just wouldn't work in this pile of stone."

He took off a headset and flipped a switch.

"...tote was on the bed. She doesn't go far without it. She has to be in the chateau somewhere."

It was Chris. Taylor lifted her head and listened.

"They saw her on Marta's back fire-escape less than thirty-minutes ago. No one saw her leave the grounds."

Lars. Taylor identified.

"Why would she go back to the tombs?"

Adie.

Where's Laszlo?

"She remembered something. Wanted to check again, perhaps."

Lars again.

"Not without her tote. Her flashlight is still in it."

Chris.

Batteries are dead, darling.

Laszlo should remember that.

Where is Laszlo?

Still talking to the three remaining terrorists?

Did he go to his room?

Will he know you were there?

"There is no place else to look." It was Lars again. "Get the torches, I will call Laszlo and tell him to bring more help."

"Right, get the men in the vineyard over here, too. If she's not hurt I'm going to throttle her. Either way I'm putting her on the first plane home," Chris said.

There was the sound of the thick door closing.

Taylor sagged.

Too late.

See what happens when you give in to curiosity.

First plane for home would be nice.

Next time behave yourself.

What next time?

Taylor felt light-headed. At the same time her body weighed a ton. It was difficult to keep upright in the chair, she felt gravity pulling her toward the floor.

"You see how convenient it has been," Piet sneered. "Now we give them a few moments to begin their search.

Then we take our walk, quick before the Russian can come with help, ehh?"

It's up to you.

Run. When you get outside run.

Oh sure. I'll be lucky to stand up.

Only way.

Taylor took slow, deep breaths, forced her mind to warm beaches and lines of clear teal surf showing off its best white lace.

Don't want to die now.

When it had been quiet in the great room for several minutes, Piet motioned her to her feet. It took every ounce of inner force, shoving, pulling, lifting together, to get her out of the chair. Each step down the hall and across the studio past the shrouded faux sculpture was a major feat. Through the French doors Taylor could see the drizzle had cleared off. When Piet opened the door she smelt the clean washed scent of the garden and took in a giant gulp of the sweet air. The hard gun muzzle pushed once more into her ribs.

Going to leave bruises.

Only if you live that long.

Taylor stepped out onto the porch.

A strong hand grasped her arm and yanked her to the right, away from the door and against the wall. There were shots, and shouts and in her ear the sound of a well loved heartbeat.

"Are you really going to throttle me?" she asked, hanging stubbornly on to consciousness.

"Quite possibly. Though you already look pretty awful."

"You do say the sweetest things. Got my tote?"

"How'd you know?" Taylor demanded as soon as she'd had a pill and a little time to re-establish her emotional and physical balance.

She was sitting on the sofa, snuggled into her husband's side, sipping on a tall glass of lemonade. Outside Laszlo was in the process of departing with a sullen, but only slightly wounded Piet.

"The cook, so he tells us," Chris told her. "He went out a back door when the shooting began. They found him huddled behind a tree. His story is he was forced to come here, and is more than happy to talk. Claims they are holding his family hostage. We traded him a promise of safety for his family in exchange for the full story. According to him, his employers were not of a nature to be discreet in front of the help. He knew quite a lot including that the chateau had been bugged, and who'd done the bugging. Needless to say, when we learned about Piet we left the cook chatting with a couple of our Swiss and Italian friends and got back here as fast we could. And, by the way, you must remind me never to tell Lars to step on it again. He drives like a mad man."

"That was very good of him," Taylor said. "Piet was going to take me for a walk by the river. How'd you know we'd come out the front?"

"Didn't. Laszlo was in the tunnel, Lars by the back door. We had you covered. And, we have fried much bigger fish than we set out to catch. Billions of dollars taken out of the terrorists' hands and several key players out of the game — all in all a huge success. How are you doing? Sure you don't want the doctor?"

"I'm fine. Now. Only, please, can we skip the fried cheese?"

CHAPTER 37

Taylor woke to the aroma of caramelized onions and braising beef. It had not been a long nap but night had fallen. Disoriented at first she soon realized she was on the sofa in the great room. A roaring fire the sole provider of light at this end of the room, at the kitchen end all lights blazed and Adie and Marta were busily employed.

"Hey," Chris said from where he sat in what she'd begun to think of as Lars' chair, working on his laptop. "Feeling better?"

"Absolutely. Where's Lars and Laszlo, you haven't misplaced them I hope?"

"Due back in time for dinner. They had a few more questions for our so called cook."

"I thought you said he was helpful."

"Too helpful, especially if he were a cook and worried about his family at home. One of the little things Laszlo learned during his week of bed rest was that security was very tight – no household help of any sort. His guards grumbled about having to take their turn at cooking, even joked among themselves that it would be more punishment to make him eat the cooking than the bread and water."

"So, this cook gave up Piet in order to cover his own involvement. It's always amazing how really sneaky some nasty people can be."

Taylor stretched and took a deep breath.

"Dinner smells wonderful. Is Piet Piet's real name by the way?"

"Unlikely."

"And Lars and Laszlo have gone to tell the pretend cook the jig is up?"

"After they've pushed him to reveal as much as possible, until then they're his best pals and full of promises. When the occasion calls for it, we, too, can be sneaky. I have, by the way, just booked us on a train to the airport and a plane home. I plan on spending the next six months revising the chapters on money trails and regaining my tan. We leave Saturday, Petra's funeral is Friday afternoon."

"So soon. The doctor decided it was an accident then?"

"After we informed him we had evidence the body had recently been found at the bottom of the shaft and moved, yes."

It was a quiet service. When the small casket of polished wood had been placed in the family crypt on a sunny mountainside they returned to the chateau — a stately parade of the ubiquitous black sedans — for coffee, wine, and pastries.

"I am suing the government," Edward informed Taylor as he filled her glass. "They have confiscated the estate of the owner of the other chateau. Our family property has been invaded, damaged, and we should be compensated."

He did not wait for her comment but continued on around the room.

"Will such a suit achieve anything?" Taylor asked.

"Edward is too thrifty to do it if it would not," Marta replied smiling. "He expects the government to settle by giving us, Edward really, the ruined chateau. Then he will organize projects: archeologists, students of architecture and ancient stone building, historical preservationists, to rebuild it as it was originally. With indoor plumbing and electricity of course."

"I told him this morning I wish to remodel the studio and live here with Marta and Adie and he actually agreed," Elsbeth said, obviously pleased at the prospect. "Edward will have his chateau and so leave us alone in ours."

"Until he decides to reopen the tunnel," Adie said, but she sounded more proud than putout.

Taylor chuckled.

So much to be happy about.

Edward is going to be too busy to mix into his sisters' lives.

Elsbeth has her life back.

All those billions of dollars that won't be buying weapons and supporting terrorists.

Laszlo found.

And Petra.

Good friends to remember.

Good food to remember.

Swiss memories.

Deadly Memories

But no fried cheese.

And in the morning, a train, a plane, and home.

Other Books by Amanda Glenn

The Taylor Books

Triangle – Dying in Mexico
Connections – Dead on Arrival
Waves – Dangerous Dancing
Pyramid – Missing in Cancun
Boxes – Death on the Intercoastal
Spirals – Deadly Memories
Kaleidoscope – Warning Lights
Triptych – Little Boy Lost
Tangled – Is She Dead Yet?
Circles – Where the Bodies are Buried
Focus – Death Scene

The Teddy Books

Pushing up Purple Daisies
Something in the Corner
Not a Suspicious Death
At the Bottom of the Garden
Death's Doorbell
They Call it a Murder
Trillium Trouble

Some Body
Tester's Ghost
I Found the Body

GTC – Good 'til Canceled

Fenner/Curtis Letters Vol I 1836-1852
Fenner/Curtis Letters Vol II 1863-1856

Eight Fables and an Essay

Books written as Glenn Specht

Darkout
Darkout – JVIII
Darkout – The Moon and Mars
Darkout – A Distant Light
Darkout – Meltdown

Hope you enjoyed the book.

glenn4amanda@Gmail.com